six Months

BL Maxwell

Six Months

BL Maxwell

Editing provided by: Pinny's Proofreading

Proofreader: Anita Ford

Warning

Intended for a mature an 18+ audience only. This book contains material that may be offensive to some and is intended for a mature, adult audience. It contains graphic language, explicit sexual content, and adult situations.

Six Months

Quinton Thorn has always wanted to own a bakery and share his love of food with as many people as possible. His passion for taking regular recipes and turning them into something special is what makes his food unique. When he meets Enzo Reid the first day of culinary school, he has no reason to question why he's there. He accepts that Enzo is just as passionate about baking as he is. He soon realizes he has feelings for Enzo that go beyond friendship, but for the sake of their business, he keeps his feelings to himself.

Enzo Reid started culinary school, hoping for a second chance. He'd already had one career, and when it disintegrated, he wanted a new start. He never meant to deceive Quinton, but he was never totally honest with him either, and now his actions will force him to choose between keeping their friendship or continuing their business. He has six months to decide what he'll do, then he'll need to live with his decision, and the choices he's made in the past.

One

Quinton

"Let's start a business together," he said.

"It'll be fun," he said.

"It won't affect our friendship," he said.

He was wrong. It hadn't been a year, and already I was itching to jump ship. It wasn't fun, and it definitely had affected our relationship.

Enzo Reid and I had been friends for a few years. We met while we were in culinary school, learning how to bake all sorts of sweet confections—yes, I, Quinton Thorn, was a baker. We both were. And we both loved the job but hated the business side of it all.

"Hey, Q, come on, man. We need to finish these donuts. We'll be opening in twenty minutes, and you know how the regulars get when we're not ready for them," Enzo called out to me from the front, where he was stocking the display cases in preparation for the morning rush.

"I'm moving as fast as I can. I can't make them cook any faster than they're cooking," I snapped back at him.

"Whatever, dick," he said, just loud enough for me to hear.

"What was that, Enzo? I thought I heard you say something." I cupped my hand to my ear like I needed help to hear what he'd said. He turned to look at me, annoyance followed by something that looked like pure hate crossing his features for a moment, then he shook his head and went back to stocking the case.

I flipped the donuts cooking in the fryer, then prepared the tray and wire rack that would hold them while they drained and cooled. I left them on the rack while I mixed the glaze and gathered all the other toppings I'd need. I was so involved I didn't notice Enzo was now standing behind me until I stepped back into him. He put his hands on my hips to steady me, and I immediately stepped away from him.

He held his hands up in surrender. "Sorry, I didn't mean to startle you. I just wanted to see if you needed any help."

"I've got it. Go set up the drawer or start the coffee." He gave me another look then: sadness. I knew this constant bickering was getting to him, but I couldn't seem to stop. And neither could he. "I'm sorry. Look, just go—"

"It's fine," he said as he turned and walked away to the other side of the shop.

I shook my head, turned back to the task at hand and started dipping the donuts in the glaze, followed by various toppings. My mind wandered back to two years ago when we'd just met. We were both so excited to learn more about baking and try our luck in the culinary world. I remember our first conversation like it was yesterday.

I noticed Enzo before he said a word. "Hey, is this the right room for Introductory Culinary Skills?" His dark brown hair, sun-kissed skin, and bright green eyes stood out when I first spotted him down the corridor.

"I hope so, I'm just starting the course. How about you?"

"Same, name's Enzo," he said, offering me his hand, dark brows arched in expectation.

"I'm Quinton. Quinton Thorn."

"Nice to meet you. Been cooking long?" he asked.

"As soon as I was tall enough to see over the counter," I said with a laugh, which he returned.

"Sounds familiar. Other kids were out riding their bikes and I was inside learning how to make piecrust."

Just then the door opened and a man in chef's whites stood holding it open for us. "Okay everyone, come on in. Let's get started."

And so began the first of many days spent together learning every aspect of professional cooking, baking, and running a business. Eventually it would become a great friendship. We worked together on most projects and assignments, and after two years—and mastering any sort of sweet treat imaginable—we graduated.

"So, I know we talked about starting a business together, I mean we've even made up a mock business plan. But what would you say if we really try it?" Enzo asked. We were sitting at a coffee shop that weekend, discussing the previous week.

"I'm not sure, they say not to start a business with a friend or relative. It can destroy a relationship, and I like having you as a friend."

"That won't happen with us. We have such a great idea with the donut place, and I can't imagine attempting it with anyone but you," Enzo said.

"We do have a great idea, and we work really well together. I just don't want to ruin our friendship," I said again. This was a huge decision and I didn't want to jump right into it.

"Come on, Q, it'll be fun." A slow smile spread on his lips, and he looked up at me from under his long lashes.

I hesitated a moment longer before I answered. "Let's do it. We'll need to look for a location, and somehow finance it."

And we did. Within eight months we were open. We found a great location in a strip mall, and using our original plan, we opened Full of Holes, our specialty donut place and bakery.

I blinked back to the present. "Remember when we first opened," I yelled over to Enzo. He looked back over his shoulder at me from the display case he was loading.

"Yep, I remember." He froze then and turned around. "What's going on, Q?"

"Nothing, just thinking." He stared at me for a second before moving back to finish loading the display case.

"Less thinking, more doing would be an excellent thing right now."

"I gotcha, Enz, we'll be ready for the morning rush." I smiled over at him, but he didn't look back or even acknowledge I'd said anything. It made me melancholy for the times we'd work together and have fun.

"Almost done with those donuts?" he called to me, once again without sparing me a second glance.

"Yeah, I'll bring them right over." Truth be told, when I first met Enzo, I had hoped maybe we could be more than friends, but I'd known him long enough now to know he wasn't interested in me. I dated other guys, but I still felt like I had a placeholder on my heart for him. *You're so stupid*, I admonished myself as I finished organizing the fresh donuts in a display tray and carried them over to put in the case.

Two

Enzo

I was such a dick. I tried being nice to Quinton, but every time I did I could see the hope bloom in his eyes. I knew he was attracted to me, but he didn't have any idea I felt the same way. He also didn't know there was no way in hell I'd throw myself back into another relationship that would eventually go to shit. They always did.

When we met at school, I had just moved here from Seattle. I was looking to start my life over again and culinary school seemed to be just the thing. I'd always baked with my mom, but I'd had a tech job in Portland. I worked in game development at one of the larger gaming companies.

I'd known Q for nearly four years, and he still didn't know what had driven me here, or why I'd needed to start over. And if it was up to me, he never would.

"Q, you got the last of the donuts ready?" I knew I sounded like a total asshole. He was always friendly and pleasant to me, but there was nothing that could make me drop the walls that had taken me years to build around my heart.

"Yeah, I just put them in the case. We're good to go if you want to go unlock the front door. I'll get going on the dishes."

I brushed past him as I walked out front to do just that. There were a few people waiting already, anxious for their caffeine and breakfast. I held the door open for them as they filed in.

"Morning, everyone, what can I get for you?" And so another day began. I didn't check to see what Quinton was doing. Whatever it was, I knew I'd made him feel uncomfortable once again with my shitty attitude. It was better in the long run. If I kept him at arm's length, then neither of us would be hurt in the end. I didn't *want* to hurt him, but I would never go through the shit I'd gone through ever again.

I rushed around, bagging and boxing donuts, croissants, muffins, and cinnamon rolls, barely staying ahead of the rush. Until I couldn't do it alone any longer.

"Q, I need some help out here." The water shut off, and he was at my side in a second, wiping his hands on his apron. He moved close as he squeezed past me. I cringed, moving away and pouring a cup of coffee for the customer I was helping.

He didn't seem to react, but I knew every time I was shitty to him, it hurt him. He was such a sweet guy, but that didn't matter—I wouldn't fuck up the second chance I'd been given to start a successful business.

"Here you go, enjoy those chocolate chip muffins, they're my favorite," he said as he handed the next customer her order. I stepped back over to the espresso machine and started on her latte. We worked so seamlessly together, he helped exactly where I needed him to. And I did the same for him.

I was lost in thought as we worked together to make sure every customer was served and on their way. We had just finished, and Quinton was wiping down the front counter, checking the napkins and stirring sticks.

"Enzo, I'm sorry if I made you uncomfortable earlier," he said to me over his shoulder.

"When? Oh, you didn't," I lied.

"Really?" he said as he turned to face me. "Because you flinched like I'd burned you, and all I did was put my hands on you to move past. I didn't mean anything by it."

"I know you didn't," I snapped, not even able to meet his eyes. He crossed his arms and stared straight at me until I turned to face him. "What? What's going on, Q?"

"Fuck you," he mumbled under his breath as he moved past me toward the back.

"Fuck me?" I said back to him, a little louder than I should have.

"Yeah, fuck you. I'm tired of walking on eggshells around you." He rushed back to stand in front of me. "I have tried everything in my power to get along with you, but you've become so fucking touchy the past few weeks I can't take it anymore."

I deflated at his words. His frustration was clear in the sad expression on his face, despite his harsh words. "I'm sorry," I said, dragging my hands through my hair.

"You keep saying that, but nothing ever changes. I don't want to work with you anymore, Enzo, it's not fun like it used to be."

"What are you saying?" I whispered, not taking my eyes off his.

"I'm saying I don't want to work with you. You work the mornings and I'll take the afternoon shift. If that doesn't work, then we'll talk about what comes next. But for now I can't keep working with you, worrying about every fucking move I make." His face was red, and he obviously struggled to keep his voice down, but his frustration was obvious. I really was a dick.

I reached my hand out to touch his arm, but he pulled away from me. "I'm sorry, I know I've been a dick, but you don't have to change your schedule. I know it works best for you."

"It doesn't matter, all that matters is not being pissed off every fucking day. I'm over it, Enzo." He stormed back to the kitchen, and the sound of pans being thrown into the sink echoed through the bakery.

I stood where I was for a few seconds, unable to move. I knew eventually I'd screw up our arrangement, and this was the day. I could tell by the look on his face and the finality in his voice—this was it. Our friendship would never be the same.

Three

Quinton

I finally snapped. It had been a long time coming, but when it happened, I realized how right it felt. I had never been someone who let myself be taken advantage of, but this day I saw everything through a different view. I would no longer make excuses for Enzo snapping at me—oh, he must be tired, he's stressed. He was a dick. None of it mattered. All that mattered now was me keeping my self-respect. He had flinched away from me like I was intentionally trying to make him uncomfortable when all I was doing was moving past him.

I finished cleaning up the kitchen and went back to the office and pulled up the schedule. It pissed me off even more that I'd be the one who had to change a schedule that I loved, just to accommodate someone who didn't really seem to care about anything other than having his way. I looked at the schedule and realized there wasn't a lot of flexibility; most of our employees were students and had to work around their classes.

I didn't want anyone else to suffer for my need for a break from Enzo, so I decided it'd be easier for me to work late at night. I'd start around eight in the evening and continue until about four in the morning. I might overlap with Enzo, but I wouldn't be working my whole shift with him. And if needed,

I'd start earlier so I could be finished earlier. Whatever it took to not be with him any more than necessary.

When we started this business, we both had the same mindset, at least I thought we did. Maybe I was wrong, because he didn't seem happy to be a business owner at all. He complained about the early shifts, and when he could plainly see I was doing my best on a task, he'd snap at me to hurry and get it done. I'd always dreamed of owning a bakery, but I didn't want to be miserable the whole time. What we had been doing didn't work, and I wouldn't go along with it. Not anymore. I didn't ask Enzo if my new schedule worked for him. I'd do what I thought was best for me from now on.

I walked through the front of the shop and out the door, not looking back to see if Enzo even noticed I'd left. He'd know eventually what I was doing. I walked to my car and drove home. I needed to sleep. I'd be starting work again in a few hours. This would be a long-ass day.

It felt like I'd just laid down when my alarm went off, and I dragged my ass out of bed and showered. I hadn't had time to think objectively about what had happened earlier, and now I realized I really didn't want to think about it. I had done nothing wrong.

I showered, dressed, and was ready to go. As I stepped out the door, I stopped for a moment. What if Enzo was still there? Logic told he me wouldn't be—he'd worked the same shift I had earlier, yet here I was going back to work only a few hours later. All to avoid someone I'd felt drawn to for reasons I couldn't even fathom at this moment.

I arrived at the bakery just as the place was closing; we stayed open until early evening for anyone craving a dessert and a late coffee. Dave, the only employee on, gave me a funny look as I walked through the door.

"Hey, what are you doing here so early?" he asked.

"Hey, Dave, this is my new shift. I'll be working eight to two, or three, or whenever I'm done."

"O-kay. I thought you liked your shift?"

"I did, but things have changed and I won't be working that shift anymore. Is that a problem?"

"Nope, no problem for me. Just wondering, that's all."

I nodded and continued through to the kitchen. After tying on an apron, I got busy weighing out the flour and other ingredients for donuts. Then I had a thought—I could make whatever the fuck I wanted to make. I could start being more creative and not worry so much about how Enzo would react. A slow smile spread on my lips at the thought. I'd always wanted to try some different recipes. Why not start now?

I leaned on the counter and thought for a second—it was spring, what was a recipe that would work well for spring? I walked over to the refrigerator to look for inspiration. Suddenly it came to me, and I mixed up the batter and carefully piped out the small circles. While they baked, I mixed the fillings, in all the colors of the rainbow to match their counterparts in the oven. When I was finished, I admired how beautiful the mini macarons looked, all lined up by color. I sampled a few, and they tasted wonderful. They'd make a great addition to our menu. To *my* menu. From now on I'd do what made me happy, and part of that was baking what recipes I thought were appropriate. I had as good a sense of these things as Enzo did, and it was about time I started proving that. To Enzo, and to myself.

I had everything ready for the day around 3:00 a.m. The time had flown by, and I knew Enzo would arrive soon. I waited until I heard his key in the door, and when he started to walk back to the kitchen, I brushed past him on my way out.

He stopped and stared at me, but I didn't stop long enough to look directly at him.

In the blink of an eye, I was out the door and I could breathe again. He'd taken away a small part of my creativity, and I was about to take it back.

Four

Enzo

That was the last shift I'd worked with Quinton—he never came in early for his evening shift, and I never stayed late. It had been weeks since we'd talked face-to-face, and I think he was happier this way. At least he didn't have to try to avoid me at work now we were never on shift together.

The other employees noticed something wasn't right between us and asked me about it constantly. I wondered if they asked Quinton too, but I was too afraid to know the answer.

I arrived at the bakery early as usual and started prepping for the day. It still felt odd to me, working alone rather than with Quinton. I weighed out the flour and started mixing the dough for cake donuts. As they finished baking, the door unlocked and Andrea stepped in.

"Hey, Mr. Reid," she called from the front.

"Morning, Andrea." I took the last of the donuts out of the oven, and while they were cooling I mixed the glaze. This batch was chocolate. Andrea walked past me and slipped her apron on. "Glad to see you finally using the key I gave you."

"Morning, should I load the cases?" she said, ignoring my comment.

"Yes, the muffins and scones on the counter are all ready to go."

"Okay," she said with a smile. She was a great employee, barely out of high school, and working for the summer to earn extra money for college. One of the few people who didn't seem to mind the early start time.

I glazed the donuts and added various sprinkles to them, just like Quinton did. That thought made me smile. I had to admit, I missed him.

"What are you smiling about?" Andrea asked me.

"Huh? Oh, nothing. Just glad I'm nearly done."

"You guys and sprinkles. I thought it was Mr. Thorn that liked to use all the different ones?"

I looked down at the donuts and the splash of color I'd created. Yep, I'd done it exactly how he would have. *What the hell?* That was one thing that annoyed me about him: always trying to be clever rather than just getting it done and keeping it simple. And, hypocrite that I apparently am, had done the same thing.

"These are ready." I pushed another tray of baked goods her way, ignoring her question. She smiled and continued until everything was ready for the day.

I went through the motions just like I did every morning, except Sunday. That day Q was on morning shift. I had to admit I really did miss him. He made work fun, and he was so inspired that it was exciting to be there when he came up with one of his crazy creations that worked, even when it annoyed me.

"Are we putting these out?" Andrea asked.

My eyes followed where she indicated, and I saw a tray I had yet to notice. Lined up neatly and ready to be put in the case were dozens of mini macarons. They were in all the colors of the rainbow and looked delicious. "Sure, Quinton must have made these."

"They're so pretty, I almost hate the idea of people eating them," Andrea commented as she put them neatly into the case.

"They are, he's so artistic. It's always fun to see what he comes up with." I tried not to smile but couldn't hold back.

"Did you two go to culinary school together?" Andrea asked.

I paused for a moment before answering. "Yeah, we did. We met there on our first day of class."

"Cool, you two are both so original. You must have had a lot of fun in school together."

"We did, he certainly made it more bearable. But sometimes we drove each other crazy, too." Remembering that time in our lives made me feel even worse about our stupid fight. I couldn't believe we'd let it go this long. Or that I started it all over something so stupid, something he had no way of knowing about because I hadn't told him.

"Was it tough getting through the classes?" she asked.

I knew she was nervous about starting school, but I had every faith she'd do great. "It was, but we made it through. Just like you will. You'll probably do even better than we did," I said, trying to reassure her.

"I'm not so sure. I mean, I did okay in high school, but college seems so much harder."

"Andrea, you were a straight-A student. I'm pretty sure you got this."

She laughed at that and walked back to the front of the shop. "Ready to open up?" she asked.

"Go ahead, we're as ready as we can be." The only thing that would make today have a better start would be working with Quinton by my side again. But I'd ruined any chance of that.

Five

Quinton

It had been a few weeks since I'd started working my late-night shift. I liked the fact that I could do whatever I wanted as far as recipes, but I did missed working with Enzo. Not enough to change my schedule, but it was in the back of my mind.

I kept busy mixing the usual doughs and recipes for the coming day. The new items I'd added to the menu seemed to be selling pretty well, and I had to admit it was fun trying out new recipes and just throwing them out there to see how our customers reacted.

The bad part of this shift was the constant weariness. I'd get home just late enough that I'd feel the need to go to bed, but I'd be so amped up from work that I'd lay there for a few hours before finally passing out, barely getting enough sleep before my alarm went off to start all over again. It still was easier than working with Enzo, though.

One good thing about working these hours was I had time to think, and I thought a lot. I knew we couldn't avoid each other forever and still own a business together, so I'd made a decision last night. But now I needed some advice.

I turned my alarm off and scrubbed at my face, hoping a shower and some coffee would wake me up. After I finished showering and was sitting with my second cup, I picked up my phone and dialed.

"Dad? I need some advice." My dad didn't pull any punches, and he didn't beat around the bush. I knew I could be blunt, and he'd appreciate it more than me wasting his time.

"Hey, Q, good morning. What can I help you with on this beautiful spring day?" His warm hello made me smile and gave me the confidence to ask him for the advice I needed.

"I'm wondering what you'd think of me buying out Enzo, or selling to him so I can start a place of my own. Preferably somewhere far away from him."

"I'm sorry things have taken a bad turn. You know I'll help you any way I can. You need to decide what you'd rather do, though. Do you want to keep the business? Or start over somewhere else? Whatever you decide, I'm behind you, and I'll do whatever you need me to."

"Thanks, Dad, I think it's been coming for a while. We've been avoiding each other for weeks, and I just can't stand walking on eggshells around him. He's always on edge and always a dick."

I heard a deep sigh come through the phone. "You can't work under those conditions, it's not fair. I'm glad you're not willing to compromise your happiness for the sake of a business. Take some time and think about it. When you come to a decision, let me know, we'll go from there. I know you've hoped for more with Enzo, I'm really sorry to hear it's turned out this way."

"Me too, Dad."

We finished catching up, and the rest of the morning flew by. I did a load of laundry, cooked a quick meal, and as I was sitting in front of the television, eating my stir-fry, I made up my mind. I would confront Enzo tonight. I wanted him to know exactly how serious I was. So far, he'd made all the decisions—that ended today.

I made a list of pros and cons on buying the business as opposed to selling it. I realized I'd rather keep it, but only if he wasn't involved in any way. I loved the location and the employees, but if he wouldn't go for it, I'd sell my share to him and start over. Even if I had to move.

I hadn't wanted to consider moving out of the area, and deep down I wanted to stay local. There were plenty of places outside of Sacramento I could start a new business—Folsom, Roseville, even West Sacramento, the possibilities were almost endless. The more I thought about it, the more excited I became. I started looking for different recipes online, hoping to find some new inspiration. There was plenty out there, and soon I had a few recipes bookmarked to try.

I finally decided it was now or never. Enzo was still working and the lunch rush had ended. He'd be preparing to leave soon. It was still early for me to go in, but once this was out in the open, it'd be a relief. I wanted to get it over with. Then I could start working toward making the most of what came next. And I could put my feelings for someone who did not care behind me. I was ready for a more serious relationship. Once the business was all taken care of, I wanted someone to share it with. Someone who'd be excited to share my accomplishments, not someone who was in a constant state of pissed off.

My mind made up, I walked out the door and braced myself for the conversation I was about to have.

Six

Enzo

"Hey, Enzo, we need to talk," Quinton said as he walked past me to the office. I was so shocked to see him, I was frozen in place for a second before I could react.

"I'll be right there." I wiped my hands on my apron, suddenly nervous. I was never nervous around Quinton before, not until I was a complete dick and he called me on it. I walked into the office where he was sitting at the desk waiting for me. "So, what's—"

"I want out, I don't want to be in business together anymore," he blurted out, not meeting my eyes.

"What? What are you saying?"

"I'm saying I want out. I'm moving out of Sacramento. I need a new start and I can't do that here." He still had not looked directly at me.

"Quinton? Why would you want to do that?" I could barely get the words out of my mouth. My throat tightened and my eyes started to burn. "We're partners, how will I run the place without you? I don't *want* to run the place without you. This was our dream."

"It was, but not anymore. I'm so fucking tired of walking on eggshells around you. You don't talk to me, you barely acknowledge me, but as soon as I tell you I'm leaving you're concerned?"

"I don't want you to leave."

"Is that just because you don't want to run the business alone?"

Quinton finally met my eyes, and the hurt that I saw in his made me gasp. "No, you're my best friend. I can't do this without you. I don't want to try." I knew I sounded desperate, but I was. I didn't want to lose him as a partner, but the thought of losing his friendship nearly made me want to puke.

"I'm done. I talked to my dad, he said I should give you time to come up with the money to buy me out. I'll give you six months, then I'm out," he said, sounding more final than I would have expected.

"Six months? Wait, are you going to stay here for six more months?" I knew I sounded frantic, but I was near panic. How could this work?

"I'll stay for six months. Then you either buy me out or put the place up for sale. I can't do this anymore."

I nodded my head more to myself than him. He was right; this didn't work. We were both miserable, and it was all on me. "Okay, Q, whatever you need. I'll start looking into a loan to buy you out. I don't want you to leave. This place was our dream . . ."

"No, it was my dream." He stood and walked to the door. "I wanted you along for the ride because I loved you." Without turning around, he walked out the door, and I was so shocked, it was a full minute before I could move. By the time I made it to the kitchen, he was already at the door. "Quinton, wait," I called, but it was too late. He was out the door. I bolted to follow him and flung the door open, but he was nowhere to be seen.

I stood there outside the door for a second, scanning the street for him. When I didn't see him, I sprinted for where he usually parked. I slid around the corner of the building just as he was closing the door to his car.

"Quinton, wait," I yelled as I ran up to the car and tapped on his window. He didn't look at me and kept his head bowed. He looked so defeated and so sad. I had done that to him. "Can we talk?" I asked. I knew I sounded desperate, but none of that mattered right now.

He looked up at me and his eyes were glassy. I'd never seen him cry, not in all the years I'd known him, yet I could tell he was right on the edge of breaking down.

I opened the door and squatted down close to his seat, taking his hand in mine. I hoped I could get through to him. "What you said in there? Is it true?" I asked, almost afraid to know the answer.

He only nodded and looked down again. "I can't do this anymore," he whispered. "You hurt me every day that we're together, and even more when we're not together. None of it seems to bother you, and you don't seem to realize how I feel about you. I can't handle it anymore." A tear slowly trailed down his cheek, and he pulled his hand from mine to wipe it away.

"Q, I had no idea you felt this way—" I started, before he cut me off.

"Didn't you? I never hid my feelings for you, but you never let me in. You don't talk to me, you keep everything to yourself. It's all about 'Enzo,' and keeping those walls up that you've painstakingly built around your heart. I don't know what happened to you in the past, but I'm the one who's been paying for it."

I couldn't speak, he had rendered me speechless. He was right. I hadn't told him anything about my past. He only knew me from the day I started culinary school, and I offered no information explaining why I'd decided to go. All while I knew everything about him. He'd gladly shared all of his past with me. I really was a shitty friend.

"Can we go somewhere and talk, I don't want to lose you as a friend. I know I haven't shown it, but you're the most important person in my life. You're all I have, Quinton."

He thought about it for a second before he answered. "No, I'm done. I can't let you hurt me any more than you already have. Bye, Enzo." He reached for the door and shut it as he turned the key. I scrabbled at the handle but he'd locked his door. I could only stand there and watch as he drove off, taking a big piece of my heart with him.

Seven

Quinton

I'd done it, I'd told him exactly what I had planned, and more importantly, exactly how I felt. He was slowly killing me with his bad attitude and micromanaging. I had hoped it wouldn't come to this, but I was so relieved to have it all out there. I couldn't believe I let it slip how I felt about him, though.

He looked shocked, like he really had no clue. I didn't see how that could be. I had made my feelings very clear on many occasions and was shot down every time. It was confusing and emotionally exhausting. He eventually made me feel like he didn't think I was good enough for him. I wondered, not for the first time, what had happened to him that would make him push me away.

I'd seen the way he looked at me when he thought I wasn't looking. The longing in his eyes was easy to see. But as soon as I would give him an opening to try to have more with me, he'd shut down and pretend to not have any idea what was going on.

I could barely see the road through the tears that wouldn't seem to stop falling now they'd started, so I pulled into the parking lot of a grocery store and stopped trying to fight them. I cried for all the times I'd hoped that Enzo would finally see me the way I saw him, and for starting a business with him that would become another statistic.

There had to be a way to make it work, so we could both be happy. I needed to live for what made me happy, though, and stop worrying so much about pleasing him. I'd done that for two years. Now t was my turn to be happy.

I wiped my eyes and looked through my phone at the recipes I'd bookmarked earlier, and decided I had nothing to lose if I tried them. I started the car and drove toward my house, but a few blocks down was a farmer's market, and I pulled over and walked through the different stalls.

Sacramento was known for its superb produce, and this farmer's market was loaded with many excellent finds. Since it was spring, there were many booths with fresh strawberries. One of them caught my eye, and I stopped to look.

"How much are your strawberries?" I asked the guy standing behind a table piled high with flats of strawberries so fresh, there were still blossom petals sprinkled throughout them. The smell of the fruit was so mouthwatering, I couldn't resist.

"Oh hey, they're fifteen dollars per flat, or you can have half a flat for ten dollars."

"They look and smell so fresh."

"They are, I just picked them this morning. They're at their peak right now."

"You sold me, I'll take two flats. If I have any left over from the recipe I have planned, I'll eat them myself." I smiled at the thought. I could do this, I could be just as successful without Enzo as I was with him. "I don't have cash, is that going to be a problem? I can go hit an ATM."

"No problem at all." He smiled as he took my card and charged it.

"Pick which ones you want, they're all good, though."

I picked up a flat and savored their scent once again, before I stacked another flat on top. "Thanks again." I walked through the rest of the stands and bought a few more small items. By the time I was walking back to my car, I was smiling. My dad was right, I could do this.

I drove home and changed to go to work, I couldn't wait to use those beautiful strawberries in a new dessert for the bakery. I had the idea to do a pastry that used a local fruit or vegetable maybe once a month, or if I was really ambitious, once a week. A few hours ago I dreaded going into work, but now I couldn't wait.

I still had a little time to kill, so once again I scrolled through recipes, looking for something different that would highlight all the fresh produce when it was at its seasonal best. The more I thought about it, the more I loved the idea. I'd have to check out a few farmer's markets and scope out the best of the best.

I checked the clock and it was already time to go. Time had flown by while I was doing something I loved and getting more and more excited about it. I left for work still wearing a smile, and with two flats of sweet-smelling strawberries I couldn't wait to use.

Eight

Enzo

Why is the month of March considered bad luck? Something to do with Caesar? I randomly thought as I made the daily donuts. Alone as usual, and by my own doing. Quinton had told me yesterday that he wanted out—out of the business, and out of my life. He'd been waiting until I was long gone to come into work, and even though he was now staying later than he had before, I never saw him. I missed him even more than I had when he'd stopped working with me. Now I knew we were on borrowed time and I only had a limited amount before he was gone for good.

I was nearly done with the toppings on a batch of cupcakes, when Andrea walked through the door. "Morning, Mr. Reid," she said, as usual.

"Call me Enzo, Andrea."

"Whatever you say, Mr. Reid," she said with a smile.

"Okay, okay, get to work." I tried to smile and go along with her joke, but it had been hard for me to smile about anything since Quinton had made his announcement yesterday. It was March; he'd be gone by September.

We both went to work in our usual routine and opened the door for a few customers who were waiting outside. It was a cold and rainy morning and no one deserved to stand out in that. I walked back behind the counter and noticed something in the case I hadn't seen before. "Andrea, what are these?"

"I'm not sure, they were in the walk-in in the back. There was a note to put them in the case."

Funny, I hadn't noticed that, but lately I couldn't seem to focus on work. I looked at the delicate chocolate pavlova nests filled with fresh strawberries. They looked delicious, and even though it was raining out, spring was on its way. They were a perfect way to make customers think about the change of seasons.

In the first hour we'd sold nearly all of them, with people eating them immediately, or taking a few home to share. Without thinking, I sent Q off a quick text to tell him how popular they were. I didn't check my phone again until after the breakfast rush when we were prepping for lunch. But it didn't matter, he hadn't replied.

Once everything was ready, my shift was ending. I was in the office going over the books when my mind wandered back to Quinton—he'd said he loved me, like it was something so obvious I should have known it. But I hadn't. I saw his attraction to me, but love? I wasn't sure how I felt about that information. Was I glad that he loved me? Or was I pissed that I was so ignorant I hadn't seen it?

I found a piece of paper that was folded in half with my name on it tucked under the laptop. My hands shook as I unfolded it and read.

Enzo, I feel bad about how we ended things. I'm still leaving in six months, but I would rather we stay friends than enemies. I know there is so much I don't know, but I wish you had trusted me as much as I trusted you. Maybe someday things will get easier, but right now it's still really hard to be around you. I don't want you to think I hate you, because I don't. And I'm thankful for meeting you and I don't regret any of the time we've spent together, I treasure it all.

Which brings me to the business end of this note. I always let you lead on what we would serve. As you know, I love to try new flavors and taste combinations. I've decided that a few times a week I'll introduce a new menu item. If they're successful, you can continue to serve them after I leave. If they're not, feel free to dump them. Tough shit if you don't like it, I'll be gone soon enough, and you won't have to deal with me again. Just kidding. I will miss you, Enz. Let's make the most of the time we still have.

PS I meant what I said, and I always will. Q

I laughed and felt a tear slip down my cheek, and the tightness that had been in my chest since he'd driven away, loosened a little. I allowed myself to think about Quinton as someone who wasn't just my partner in business, and I liked how that felt.

I was so stupid, but then I remembered I still had five and a half months. Maybe I could make up for being such a dick all those years. That thought got me excited. What if I made the effort and showed Quinton how important he was to me and the business? Well, mostly to me. He was a wonderful man, and a great friend that I took for granted. I needed to spend every second I could attempting to fix that. Even if he still left, I needed to make it clear that I appreciated him and truly regretted how I'd treated him. I needed to be honest with him about why I kept him at arm's length. But not today, first I needed to let him know I'd read his note and appreciated it, and his extra efforts. Today, things would change for me. I only hoped it wasn't too late to make a difference.

Nine

Quinton

I couldn't believe it was already one month closer to us dissolving our partnership. I was still nervous, but I found myself more excited now. I had gotten into a routine of checking out the farmer's markets nearly every morning they were open. I had three main ones I visited that had proven to have the best produce available.

To say I could be more creative was a huge understatement. I devoted most of my time, when I wasn't working, to developing new recipes based on the incredible ingredients I was able to find. I couldn't believe we'd never thought to go to the farmer's markets before, they were such a huge resource, one I wasn't sure I'd have discovered if I hadn't been so upset after talking to Enzo.

I had also talked to my dad again, and told him I wanted to stay here. I'd put my heart and soul into this place, and while it seemed to bring Enzo nothing but stress, it brought me lots of joy. I had drawn up an offer to see if he'd be willing to sell to me. I worried about what he'd do if he no longer worked here, but as per his decision, that was no longer my business.

The thought excited me. I had so many new ideas for the bakery, I could hardly wait to try them out, and if Enzo declined my offer, I'd take my time and find a place that I loved as much as this one. Either way, I'd make my business a success.

I was not only willing to put in the time, but I was finding out I had a real talent for using the available ingredients. Lately I'd even tried making more savory treats for the lunch crowd. Today I'd be using the fresh spinach I'd bought this morning in a spanakopita recipe. The tender leaves were hard to resist. But since we didn't offer many savory treats, there were a few things I'd need to pick up before I went to work. I hoped this went over as well as I expected it would, because if it did, it could be the first in what I hoped would be hot and cold items we could serve for lunch. As it was, we mostly had the same pastries we offered for breakfast, but I liked the idea of attracting more of a lunch crowd along with the coffee crowd. Not that I didn't appreciate them, I just wanted to offer them more reasons to stop in for a treat during the day.

I also had the idea to serve breakfast sandwiches or burritos. There was a Mexican restaurant near to us. I played with the idea of asking them if they'd be interested in making burritos and selling them to us, since they didn't serve breakfast. It seemed my creative juices were flowing, and I relished in the feeling of being both creative and at peace with my decisions.

Ten

Enzo

True to form, March had come in like a lion, and was looking like it would leave like a lamb. "April is the cruelest month," said T.S. Eliot. Well, this April would be the beginning. The last part of March passed by so fast. We were so busy with Easter, and everything spring related, I didn't have much time to put into my relationship with Quinton.

But today that changed. It was now April, and I was one month closer to losing him. He'd been working so hard, introducing two more new items beside the chocolate pavlova the customers were crazy about. I should have let him do this from the start.

I still hadn't seen him. He worked late, but always made sure he was gone before I got there in the morning—even though morning was at four. Quinton had done exactly what he said he would, and he was making me regret him leaving, even before he'd gone.

"Morning, Andrea, how are you today?" I asked as she unlocked the door.

"Morning, I'm fine. What's got you in such a good mood?" she asked.

"Nothing, and everything," I answered.

"Well, whatever it is, keep it up. That smile looks nice on you."

"Thanks." I walked back to the kitchen and started bringing pastries out of the walk-in to stock the front cases. Noticing a covered tray with today's date on it, I peeked under the parchment paper and smiled. This was going to be a great day. I carried the tray out to the front, and began stocking the case with the fresh berry tarts that Quinton had made. As I carefully transferred the delicious-looking tarts to the case, I couldn't resist putting one aside to sample.

I sliced it in half, and when Andrea walked back to the kitchen, I handed half to her.

"Oh, these look so good," she said before taking a bite. "Quinton is a pastry genius. No offense, but these are fucking good." She blushed and ate the rest of the tart.

"Quinton always had a way with pastry, the crust is perfect and the filling light and creamy. We should add these as a regular on the menu," I said to myself.

"I agree, they're delicious." She walked out to finish loading the case, and I took out my phone. *The tarts are great! Let's make them permanent,* I tapped out before I could lose my nerve.

Quinton's response was almost instant: *Glad you like them, the berries were at the farmer's market and I couldn't resist. I can give you the recipe.*

That would be great, thanks again.

We were busy, but the whole time I worked filling orders and making coffee, my mind wandered to Q, and all the recipes I could think of that would bring something new to the business. There was one recipe in particular I'd wanted to try out for a while. Maybe I could whip up a batch today so Quinton could try it and I could get his opinion.

I liked to believe as my grandmother had always said: April showers bring May flowers. Her way of saying that the rain would pass, and after, the world would be beautiful for it. I realized I needed to do my part too, I couldn't just sit back and wait for things to change. I needed to be part of that change.

After the breakfast rush, I found the recipe I was looking for and started gathering ingredients. This was my grandmother's recipe, but I hadn't made it for years. It was a simple sugar-cookie dough dropped by a small scoop onto the cookie sheet. After they cooled they'd be filled with raspberry cream filling. They were light and buttery and perfect for a springtime treat.

It didn't take long for me to have a few dozen finished and in the case, ready for the lunch crowd. I set aside a few and packed them in a box. I wrote Quinton's name on it and left it on the counter before I left for the day, my own note attached to it.

Enjoy the cookies, you deserve something sweet for all the nice things you do for everyone. Sorry it took me so long to see it. Have a good night. Enzo.

I walked out the door to my car and realized I was smiling. I couldn't remember the last time I'd felt so good and not bogged down by all the responsibilities of work. It was a great feeling. Then I had a thought. Maybe I could go in a little earlier tonight and see Quinton. It had been a few weeks, and if I was being honest, I missed him more than I would have ever realized.

I walked a little faster, already planning to go to bed earlier. Why not? At this point I had nothing to lose with him. And maybe I could tell him to his face how good his new treats were doing. Yeah, that was it, I'd go in early just to make sure he knew I appreciated it. It had absolutely nothing to do with me missing him more each day.

Eleven

Quinton

I read the text from Enzo and fought not to smile at it. I was just getting ready to go to bed, but I couldn't stop thinking of other recipes to add to the inventory. Tonight I'd make the spinach spanakopita, and depending how it sold, I'd start adding more savory items. The more creative I was with food, the happier I was. I'd thought being in business with Enzo would make me happy, and it had. Until things changed. But in some ways I was happier now. I didn't have anyone telling me my ideas were no good. It was so freeing.

I climbed into bed and looked at my phone one last time before putting it beside me and falling asleep. I was so tired I didn't have a chance to dream, and after not nearly enough sleep, I woke to the sound of my phone ringing.

"Hey, Dad, what's going on?"

"Did I wake you? I'm sorry, I was hoping we could get together, maybe go out for lunch."

I stretched and wiped at my eyes as I scooted up to a sitting position. "Sure, can you give me about an hour? I need to shower first."

We made plans and I hurried to shower and dress. I loved meeting up with my dad, but I craved having someone special to share a meal with. It had been so long since I'd even gone out on a date. I needed to put myself out there. I was tired of doing nothing but working and sleeping. And worrying about Enzo.

I walked into the restaurant and saw my dad sitting at a table already. "That was fast," I said as I sat down across from him.

"I called you from here," he said with a smile.

"Did you already eat?"

"Nope, I had coffee, but I wanted to wait for you."

We caught up about our lives and all the changes that were coming. "Have you decided what you want to do yet?" he asked.

"Yeah, I have."

"Well?" He tapped the tabletop. "Don't keep me waiting, what did you decide?"

I waited for a moment before answering, not to draw it out for him, but to make sure I was still as certain about my decision. And I found I was, I was absolutely sure. "I want to keep it. I want to buy Enzo out."

He took a drink of his water and couldn't hold back his smile. "I'm proud of you, son. I know how much that place means to you. So, sounds like we need to come up with a good plan for your next move."

We sat at the restaurant and talked long after we'd finished eating, and when I left, I was more confident I'd made the right decision. I was the one who loved this work, and our place. Enzo could be the one to move on and start over. He'd done it before, and he could do it again.

It hurt me to realize that he really would be gone, but working without him hadn't been as bad as I expected it to be. I enjoyed it. I could work at whatever pace worked for me, as long as I was finished on time. And it was worth it for the creative freedom alone. I still missed him, though. He pissed me off so much, but we had done so much together the past few years, it was like something was always missing without him around.

I drove back to my house and got busy doing things I'd been neglecting since I'd been working so much, and it wasn't long before it was time to leave for work again.

I arrived just as the late crew was leaving. I waved goodbye to them, and after locking the front door, I got busy making the spanakopita. It smelled delicious as I was mixing the filling, and I couldn't resist trying a piece as soon as I took it out of the oven. It was delicious, and it would work well for breakfast or lunch. I expected it to be another hit.

I was lost in thought, thinking about what I'd be able to find at the farmer's market for the week, when I heard keys jangling in the front door. I walked forward so I could get a glimpse at who was coming in, and was shocked to see it was Enzo.

I hurried over to the mixer I'd been filling with ingredients for donuts when he moved into view. I tried to school my features and not let on how happy I was to see him. When his eyes met mine, he looked so hopeful—and nervous. He must have seen the same emotions in my expression, because he went from bright-eyed excitement to hesitant in the matter of a few seconds.

I took a deep breath and greeted him; I knew how this would all end. I just had to get through the next few months. And I *would* get through the next few months.

Twelve

Enzo

I dragged my ass out of bed and was at the bakery by half past one . . . in the morning. What was I thinking? I knew what I was thinking, maybe I could salvage a small part of our friendship that was left. The less I saw of Q, the more important I realized he was to me.

I let myself in through the front door and walked past the counter into the back. Quinton was at the large mixer, and he turned when he saw me. His eyes lit up for a moment before a cloud passed over his expression and he acted indifferent to the fact I was there.

"What are you doing here so early?"

"I wanted to come in and tell you thanks for the new pastries you've been baking. They've been very popular and—well, I just appreciate your effort," I said.

He stood there staring at me for a second, not moving and up to his elbows in dough that I'd use to make donuts in a couple of hours. "Okay, I'm glad to hear that," he said, then went back to transferring the dough to a bin so it could rise.

I walked back so I was closer to him. I needed him to understand I really meant what I was saying. "Q? I'm sorry about how shitty I've been. I don't just mean at work. I mean all the time."

He turned to face me, a look of uncertainty crossing his face. "Why now, Enzo, what's changed?" he said, crossing his arms and staring at me with fire in his eyes.

"I miss you, and your friendship." Time to be honest with him.

"Why now? You've been shitty to me for years. Is it just because I decided to not take it anymore?"

"It's because I was a shitty friend. You've always been there for me, and I took it for granted. Can we start over, try to mend our friendship over the next few months?"

"You mean before I leave?"

My face grew hot and I could feel the shame rolling off me. "Yes, but if I'm being honest, I keep hoping you'll change your mind."

"That's not gonna happen. I may stay in the area, but we're done as business partners."

"I'm so sorry." I rubbed the back of my head, barely able to meet his eyes from the guilt of how badly I'd treated him. He continued to stare at me, not letting me off easy.

"Why don't we see how things are by September? I don't want to lose you as a friend, but you don't treat a friend the way you've been treating me." His voice cracked as he swallowed and turned his attention back to the dough.

Stepping closer to him, I squeezed his hand. "I'm sorry." I hoped he could see I meant it. I had fucked this all up so bad not telling him everything before we went into business. Then I realized I had a second chance, not at being in business with him, but being the friend I should have been all along.

He nodded his head and took a deep breath before clearing his throat. "I ate the cookies, thanks for that. It was a nice surprise," he said while he moved to gather ingredients for his next creation.

"How were they?"

"Delicious, your grandma's recipe, right?"

"Yes, I can't believe you remembered that," I said.

"I remember everything, Enz, everything." He looked at me then with a shy smile.

I left him to whatever he was working on and started gathering my own ingredients for maple scones. I was chopping the pecans when I felt Quinton standing right next to me.

"What are you making?" he asked as he looked over my shoulder for a peek.

"Maple pecan scones." I smiled at him.

"My favorite."

"I know," I said as casually as I could manage.

"You remembered?" he said, his voice full of both wonder and shock.

"I did, and I'm going to pay more attention so I remember even more." He didn't say anything, just clapped me on the back and walked off toward the office.

I stayed busy, starting on my usual routine and thinking about some other new items we could try. Quinton walked out of the office and back over to the counter he'd been working at. He set a plate next to me, and instantly I was hit with the smell of garlic, cheese, and other savory spices.

"You made spanakopita?" I said as I shoved a bite in my mouth. "Oh god, so good."

"Not too much garlic?" he asked as he popped a piece in his own mouth.

I looked at him then, really looked him—his dark brown eyes, soft, curly brown hair, and his warm smile that I had missed so much—and it made me feel even worse for being so horrible to him. "It's perfect. Absolutely perfect." I meant what I said, but I didn't just mean the spanakopita.

I continued watching Quinton as he cleaned up his area and checked on the baked goods he'd made for the day, then finally he stopped and looked at me. "I want to try some savory recipes and see how they do. The regulars keep asking for more hearty foods. I thought this was a good start. Also, I talked to the Mexican place, and they said they could make us breakfast burritos no problem."

"That sounds like a great idea. A few customers mentioned it to me too. You talked to them already, huh?"

"Yeah, I wanted to get going on it," he said.

"Okay, I'll let you know how the spanakopita does. And Quinton?"

He paused and looked at me. "Yeah?"

"Great idea, thanks."

"All right, everything is ready for you to open. Have a good day, Enz," he said with a wave as he walked toward the front of the shop.

I looked up with a smile. "Thanks, you too. Go get some sleep." The last thing I heard was his laugh before the door shut behind him, and I made myself stop and just enjoy that sound and the warmth it filled me with. Suddenly it hit me—this wasn't just about losing a friend; it was about losing someone who could have been more. Someone that I looked past and didn't pay enough attention to. He deserved so much more, and by September he'd know he mattered to me.

Thirteen

Quinton

I left the shop feeling lighter than I had in weeks. Enzo made an effort to apologize, really apologize, and to say I appreciated it would have been an understatement. I still wanted out of our partnership, but if we could remain friends . . . well, I'd like that. I didn't want him as an enemy. I just didn't want to be in business with him.

Ironically, since I'd told him my plans, he'd been really stepping up his efforts. He was a great cook, but he didn't seem to enjoy it as much as he did working on his computer. Which worked out well for us when we needed help with something in the tech world, but we didn't seem to blend the two very often.

It was still too early for the farmer's market to open, but I made a stop for coffee and headed to the parking lot it was located at on this day. I sat in my car and watched as the trucks started to arrive that carried all the fresh produce at its seasonal best. I did a few Google searches for what should be at its peak this time of year, and by the time the vendors were almost done setting up their booths, I had a few recipes that would work well if I was lucky enough to find everything I needed.

"Morning."

"Morning. Hey, you were here early last week." The same man who had helped me before with the strawberries was here again.

"Yep, that was me. The berries were a big hit. I see you have more, I'll take another flat. What else is fresh?" I asked, while looking at all the fresh produce he had to offer.

"Grapes are in season, pears and cherries too."

"Not sure what I could use grapes for, but the pears and cherries I'll take." He handed me a bag, and I started picking some pears out; they smelled so sweet and were perfectly ripe. I chose about a dozen of them then picked out enough cherries for roughly six pies.

Once again, I was excited to get back to work and start baking. Using these fresh ingredients seemed to be just the change that I'd needed to get excited about food again. I wished that somehow this had happened sooner, and I could have brought Enzo along with me. I handed the guy my card, and he charged me for the fruit I'd bought. "Hey, what's your name?" I asked him.

"I'm Steve. I'm always here on Wednesday, then at a few of the other farmer's markets on the other days."

I shook his hand before I took back my card and loaded up my fruit. "Nice meeting you, Steve, you'll be seeing me regularly." He waved me off as I walked back to my car.

Once again, I thought of Enzo. He seemed so happy to see me, and he'd actually come in a few hours early to make *sure* he saw me and told me thanks. He'd never done that. Maybe he really was trying to change. I wasn't sure, but I hoped he wouldn't fight me on buying him out. He did the work now because he had to, not that he wanted to or was passionate about it. He loved baking, but not as a business. The fact that he baked his grandma's cookies for me told me a lot. He cared, he wanted to show me how thankful he was for me, and so he baked the one recipe he'd never wanted to share with the bakery. I think I understood why a little more than I had before. He was a businessman, but he let that business-minded thinking get in the way of our friendship.

I had so many questions for him, I needed more information. Maybe in the end I'd have my own business, but I'd also still have a friend. I wanted that.

I pulled up to my house and my mind wandered back to last night. I never expected Enzo to show up and apologize. If he could make that effort, then maybe I could attempt to be more honest with him too. I'd always kept my feelings for him hidden, but now that I'd blurted them out to him, there wasn't a point in denying it any longer.

I finally made my way inside, and after putting everything away, I flopped on my bed, asleep almost instantly. The late nights and long mornings of going to the farmer's markets were taking a toll on me. But I found I didn't mind. It was worth it to get such great ingredients, and it was fun too.

Tonight would be another fun night. I'd get to try another new recipe, and I couldn't wait.

Fourteen

Enzo

I continued to go in early and stay through my whole shift. Just getting an hour of time with Quinton had somehow become the highlight of my day. Even if I was in bed before dark every freaking night, it was totally worth it. I had forgotten how fun he was to be around when there wasn't so much stress hanging over us.

"I want to run something by you," I said tonight, as I brushed past him on the way to the office.

"Hello, Quinton. How are you doing, Quinton? Having a good night, Quinton?" He gave me a hard stare over the counter he was busy mixing dough on. I stopped in my tracks and walked back to where he stood.

"Hello, Quinton, how are you doing? I hope you're having a good night tonight," I said with as much enthusiasm as I could manage this early in the morning.

He rolled his eyes before he spoke again. "What did you want to show me?"

"So, I was thinking maybe we'd try taking online orders. I set up a site to show you what I mean, and to get your opinion."

"Enzo, you know we won't be partners in a few months. Do what you think is best."

The excitement that had coursed through me only a second ago was now gone. I was so stupid. I knew he was still deciding what he'd do, but I was so excited to share my idea with him, I hadn't even thought about him leaving.

I turned to walk away when a hand on my shoulder stopped me. "Show me what you got," he said.

"It's okay, I totally forgot about you leaving. I don't want to waste your time on things you're not interested in."

"Who said I'm not interested? I just don't want to make any decisions for the business that you have to live with after I'm gone. But I'd love to see what you came up with." He smiled warmly at me and pulled up a stool to the counter. "Show me what you got." He clapped both hands on the counter.

I laughed in relief as I unpacked my laptop. "It's just a rough version, but I thought maybe we could start selling a few items and see how it does. Andrea is very creative with packaging, and with your recipes and my superior web-designing skills, I thought we could try it."

I booted up the laptop and quickly found the files I wanted to show him. I'd taken a few pictures of the two of us when we'd first opened Full of Holes, and put those on the front page. Next was a menu of the different treats we would offer, which would change every few months or by the season.

He looked over each page, making suggestions and pointing out things he both loved and hated. This was what I'd missed, we worked so well on this level. He wasn't afraid to tell me when he didn't like something, but he was so excited to tell me when he loved it.

"I think it could work, Enz. You might need to hire another person to handle the online orders, though. Then you wouldn't have to stress about one more thing during the day."

"You could be right. I can see this being a fairly lucrative part of our business," I said, not realizing what I'd said until he looked away and seemed to think hard on something. "What is it?" I asked.

"You have to start accepting that our business is changing. I may be around, but not as a business partner. I need to know you understand."

My eyes burned, and my lip trembled. "I know, it's just really hard to imagine you not here."

"It'll be okay. We'll both work it out and we'll still be friends. We're working on being better friends now, right?"

I gave him a watery smile before I swallowed the lump in my throat to answer. "Yeah, we are. I don't want to lose you, Quinton. I hope you know that. I've screwed it all up, and I'm working hard to show you how much you mean to me."

"You are?" he whispered. I could only nod. We held each other's gaze for a second before he smiled and put his arm around my shoulder.

"I am," I said, and I hoped he didn't notice the tremble in my voice.

"I'm glad, Enz, you mean the world to me. You're my best friend. I—" He cleared his throat before squeezing my shoulder and pulling his arm away. "I need to finish the pie dough or it won't be ready in time for lunch."

I stood and packed up my laptop and walked into the office to put it away. On my way back out I stopped with my hand still on the door and turned back to him. He was in the exact place he had been a moment ago. "You mean the world to me too, Q. You always have." With that I walked out to the bakery to start on my duties for the morning.

As I worked by myself, I went over our earlier conversation and how easy it had always been to talk to Quinton. I also tried to figure out what had changed, and why I started treating him like he didn't matter. Guilt twisted in my gut the more I thought about all the times I'd been short or just plain dismissive of him. He'd been nothing but kind and supportive of me. Always ready to listen with interest, and to give me an honest opinion.

The longer I thought about it, the more guilt burned through me. Then I was hit with another memory from before I'd met Quinton, of sharing my ideas with another friend, and what he did with that information. I shook my head, not wanting to revisit that mess again. Ever.

Andrea unlocking the door was a great distraction from a past I wanted to forget had ever happened. "Hey, boss, ready to get to work?" she called back to me.

"Hey, Andrea. I've already been working, for hours. Why didn't you come and join me earlier?" I joked.

"I was trapped in my bed, it would not release me until sunrise."

"You need to do something about that." I winked at her.

"Nope, I'm good, this is early enough, thanks."

"Hey, I have an idea I want to get your opinion on," I said as I started once again stocking the display case for the morning.

She walked over to me, her excitement clear. "What did you come up with?"

"What's your take on internet sales?" I asked.

She smiled at me before following me back to the office to listen to the same information I'd shared with Quinton earlier. He was right, this could be amazing.

Fifteen

Quinton

Enzo had been coming in early for work since the end of June. It was now early July and he was still at it. I can't say I minded seeing him, since I missed him after I'd changed my schedule. I hoped that we continued to get along as well as we had been, I didn't care for the asshole he'd slowly become. But I had missed the old Enzo. More than I cared to let myself admit.

I finished this shift, and as I was driving home I thought about the conversation we'd had a few weeks back, about his idea for online orders. It was a good idea. I'd seen other bakeries that had done it, and it seemed to be a very successful part of their business. People did everything online, so why not order your baked goods too? The website he showed me looked great, very professional, and easy to use. I had no idea he was so good with web design. I wouldn't have known where to start.

When I arrived at my house, I set a reminder to call the Mexican restaurant to check on the breakfast burritos I'd be bringing into the bakery. Tomorrow would be the first day, and since it was nearing the Fourth of July, it was a good time to start serving a fast, and portable, breakfast. I wondered if Enzo had plans for the Fourth. We worked so many hours that neither of us usually celebrated the holiday, but this year it fell on a Sunday and we had planned to close for it.

I slept a few hours, the days without enough sleep catching up to me, but my mind not allowing me to rest for long. When I awoke, it was to the sounds of the birds singing in the trees outside my house, and the sun was just beginning to rise. It was going to be a beautiful, clear day, but already it promised to be a hot one. I turned on the air conditioner as I walked by the thermostat on the way to take a cool shower. July in Sacramento was no joke, it was usually a hundred degrees most days, and sometimes in August it would be even hotter than that. This year was no exception.

My mind wandered to the list of things I needed to do later today, one of which included picking up the breakfast order for the following morning. I checked my phone and noticed a text from Andrea.

Hey Quinton, I'm not feeling well. Is it okay if I take the day off? I know it's the last day before the Fourth but I was out at the river after work yesterday and I think I overdid it.

I replied immediately with, *Sorry to hear that, but I hope you had fun. Glad to see you getting out there and doing something besides working. No problem, I can go in earlier and help Enzo with the breakfast rush.*

Andrea's next message came as I was getting clean clothes out of my dresser drawers: *Are you sure? I know you worked last night.*

Yep, take it easy and stay cool. I'll see you in a few days.

I set my phone on top of the dresser, and after getting dressed, I hurried back to the shop. This was going to be a long-ass day, but there was no way I'd leave Enzo to do the shift alone.

I called the Mexican restaurant, and as luck would have it, someone was there already getting ready for their day. I asked if I could pick up the burrito order shortly and was told it would be ready when I got there.

They came through, as promised, and I picked up the still warm burritos and rushed to unlock the door at the bakery, balancing the bag of burritos while digging out my keys. I opened the door in a rush, and Enzo looked up at me in surprise, then I locked the door and walked back to the kitchen as he watched my every move.

He still said nothing as I tied my apron, rubbed my hands together, and waited for him to ask what was going on, and why I was here. And I realized that even though I'd be exhausted later, I was excited to be here now, with him.

Sixteen

Enzo

July was here before I could think about it. As usual Sacramento was like a fucking blast furnace. It hadn't been less than a hundred degrees in nearly two weeks. This time of year I was thankful that I worked so early in the morning, at least the ovens didn't need to be on during the day when it was already so hot.

It was still early, Quinton had left around two in the morning, but a little before six, I heard a key in the door. I looked up, expecting to see Andrea, but was surprised to see Quinton walking in.

"Hey, what are you doing back? Did you forget something?" I asked.

"Nope, Andrea messaged me, she's not feeling well. She was out yesterday in the sun and thinks maybe she overdid it. She asked if I could help you this morning."

"You didn't have to do that. I could've worked it out," I said as I walked toward him, wiping my hands on my apron.

"I know, but I don't mind. This way we'll both finish early."

"You're sure?"

"Yeah, it'll be like old times. Remember how much we worked when we first opened?"

"Oh god, I don't think I could do that again." I thought back to those first few months when it was just the two of us doing everything. It was tough, but also rewarding to know we could do it. "Hey, whatcha got there?"

"I picked up breakfast burritos from a few doors down like I suggested. If it works out, we can make them a regular thing."

"I might need to sample one, just to make sure they're up to our standards."

He laughed and slapped me on the back as he walked past, headed for the walk-in. "I'll start stocking the front, you finish what you're doing. We got this."

He was right, once we got into our rhythm, breakfast was over, the lunch crew arrived, and it was time for us to leave. The place was stocked, clean, and ready to go. As the next shift came on and I briefed them on what we had available today, and the specials, Quinton stood next to me and offered his own advice on how to price some items, and his recommendation on how to sell them.

After talking to the lunch crew, we both walked out together. "What are your plans for the day?" I asked.

"Sleep, lots of sleep."

"Oh, okay. Well, have a good day, get some rest," I said, and started to move toward my car.

"Enz, want to go out later and have a beer? We're both off tonight since tomorrow is the Fourth. Might as well make the most of it."

I stopped and turned to face him. "I could go for a beer. Maybe after you get some sleep?"

"Sounds like a date," he said as he turned to walk away. "And be prepared to go out dancing, we're going to do it right." Quinton turned back to smile before he walked around the corner of the building and out of sight.

I groaned. Maybe this wasn't such a good idea after all.

As soon as I arrived at home, exhaustion hit, and all those early mornings caught up with me. I stumbled to my bedroom and flopped facedown on my bed. I was asleep before I even had time to think about falling asleep.

I awoke a while later to the sound of my phone ringing. Without looking to see who it was, I answered. "This is Enzo."

"Hey, sleeping beauty, you ready to go out and grab a few beers?" Quinton asked, the smile in his voice clear.

I shot up, instantly awake. "Yep, when did you want to go?"

"How about now? I'm at your front door." I jumped up from my bed and walked to the door with my phone still clutched in my hand.

"Hey, come on in," I said as I opened the door. "Mind if I take a quick shower? I just woke up."

"Oh really?" Qunton teased as he took in my rumpled hair and clothes.

I gave him a shove before walking to the bathroom. After a quick shower and throwing some jeans and a T-shirt on, I was ready to go. I walked back out into the living room to find Quinton asleep on my couch, neck bent at an impossible angle that I knew would give him a kink if he slept in that position for much longer.

I shook him gently and he startled awake. "Hey, sorry. Didn't mean to fall asleep." He rubbed his eyes before stretching with a few cracks and pops. "You ready to go?" he asked as his eyes took me in from head to toe.

"Yeah, let's do this."

We decided to go to Old Sacramento, since there was a variety of bars and restaurants, and with it being a holiday weekend, it'd be hopping. We weren't disappointed. After driving around for thirty minutes we finally found a space, and slowly made our way down the wooden sidewalks to the restaurant we'd agreed on.

We walked into the small bar space and squeezed through a packed house to finally make it to the counter to place our orders. After paying and waiting for our beers, we made our way upstairs in search of a table. "This place is packed, I'm glad we got here early," I said.

Quinton led us through the crowd to a small table that overlooked the dance floor and was next to a few old arcade games. "How's this?"

"Perfect, we can play *Centipede* while we wait for our food to get here."

"Why would you want to put yourself through that?" he asked, voice full of fake concern. "I'm thinking tonight is the night I kick your ass." He wove his fingers together and stretched out his arms to make a show of cracking his knuckles.

"Not tonight, I'm feeling especially lucky. I'm thinking I can at least double your score."

"Bring it. Come on, let's play while we wait for dinner."

We walked over to the *Centipede* game and plunked in our quarters. After about twenty minutes, it was evident tonight was not my lucky night as Quinton kicked my ass for the umpteenth time at this stupid '80s game that we both loved.

Laughing and shoving each other while fighting to blast various insects, we almost missed it when they announced my name over the loudspeaker. "I'll go get our food," I offered.

"You mean you'll go get it to avoid losing worse than you already are?"

"Something like that," I mumbled as I gave him a final shove before walking downstairs to pick up our orders.

When I returned with our burgers and fries, the waitress was just leaving our table where she'd brought us both another beer.

"Perfect timing, this looks great," Quinton said as he took a drink before sampling a fry. I held out my beer in a toast.

"To friends," I said, and took a big drink.

"To friends."

We clinked our bottles together and started shoving food in our mouths. The long hours must have helped us both work up an appetite, because neither of us said much else until we were finished.

"So what do you want to do now?" I asked, just as the band started to play downstairs. A slow grin spread across Quinton's lips as he nodded in that direction.

"I can think of something," he said, before he stood and started to walk downstairs.

"Hey, wait up," I called after him, and he looked back and smiled.

By the time we got to the bottom of the stairs, the music was so loud it was impossible to talk. The beer gave me a nice buzz as I started to move to the music before I was even near the dance floor.

Quinton did the same, started to dance his way down the stairs and then across the bar area to the dance floor. As soon as I turned the corner, there was a wall of people already moving. I spotted Quinton and settled my hand on his hip as he started to really move. He clasped his hand over mine and pulled me closer to him.

We'd danced numerous times before, but somehow I never noticed how good it felt to move in close to him and breathe in his intoxicating scent. I didn't hold back as I moved in close enough for my nose to brush against his hair. When I realized what I was doing, I tried to pull my hand back, but he held firm. He didn't turn around or act like anything had happened, he just continued to dance to the music.

I relaxed slightly and stepped back into him, reaching my hand around to his stomach where he wove his fingers with mine and held it against him. I was buzzed, but I wasn't drunk, and right now, I knew something was happening, something was changing, and neither of us seemed to be strong enough to stop it. I knew that whatever happened now would change our relationship, and possibly both our lives.

With that thought, I leaned even closer into him and nuzzled my nose into his neck while he pressed back into me and squeezed my hand tighter and continued to sway to the beat.

Seventeen

Quinton

Feeling his touch on my body was everything. I wanted more and couldn't resist squeezing his hand on my stomach and pulling him closer to me. I had missed his touch more than I cared to admit. But this moment seemed different, almost like a surrender for us both. We'd gone out many times in the past, but we'd both seemed to keep ourselves in check and crossed no lines that could affect our friendship. Something in me told me that didn't matter anymore.

Enzo nuzzled into my neck and a shiver ran through me, and I felt goose bumps rise where his skin met mine even though it was hot in the press of people on the dance floor. I reached my hand back and wove my fingers through his short hair and scratched at the nape of his neck with my fingertips. He groaned in my ear and it went straight to my cock. I closed my eyes and continued to sway to the music while his lips brushed against my neck, just under my ear.

I shouldn't want anything with him. All the times he'd been shitty to me flashed behind my eyelids, and then he wove his arms around me and squeezed me tighter to him. He gently kissed my neck, his lips lingering there for far longer than I would expect, but not long enough all at the same time.

I spun around, and taking his face in my hands, I kissed him like I'd wanted to for nearly as long as I'd known him. I brushed my tongue along his lips, and he answered by sucking my tongue into his mouth. The warmth of his lips and his arms around me were all I could focus on.

He tightened his arms around me and pulled our hips together. "Take me home with you, Quinton. God, I want you so bad."

I leaned my forehead against his as the music slowly faded away. I took his hand and pulled him behind me until we were outside the restaurant.

"Come on, over this way," I said as I pulled him along. We turned at the side of the building, and finally we were alone in the dark. He leaned against the side of the building, and I wasted no time in kissing those lips I'd only imagined until tonight. "I've wanted to kiss you for so long."

He pulled back and looked me in the eye. "Why didn't you? Oh my god, Q, I've dreamed about your lips."

I huffed out a laugh and promptly continued to kiss him until we both needed to catch our breath. Even then, my fingers were hungry for his skin, and I brushed my hand under his shirt, my eyes closing at the feel of him.

"Take me home, please take me home with you," he nearly begged. Once again, I pulled back enough to look into his eyes, then nodded. I took Enzo's hand again, and we hurried to where we'd parked, neither of us able to slow down or stop touching. All I could focus on was getting him home and being alone with him. And all that beautiful skin that I couldn't wait to touch more of.

We found my car and hurried to get inside, and as soon as we were both settled and I had the car started, I reached for his hand and pulled it over to my leg. I drove with one hand on the wheel the whole way home. Neither of us said anything, but every time I looked over at him, he was already looking at me, the want in his eyes so easily on display—and all of it just for me.

I squeezed his hand tighter and drew it up to my chest. "Almost there," I said, more to myself than to him. He didn't answer, just squeezed my hand and didn't let go.

Finally, I pulled into my driveway, and waited for my garage door to open with very little patience left. I eased into the garage, and as soon as the door closed, we were both out of the car and standing in front of it. "Enz, I need to be honest with you. As soon as we go into my house, I will kiss you, and then I'm gonna want to do other things that business partners shouldn't do."

"We won't be partners anymore, remember?" he whispered, before stepping forward and taking my face in his hands. He stared deeply into my eyes. "I want this, Q, I want you." And then he kissed me the way I'd always wanted to be kissed. It was as if he was claiming me and giving me a choice, both at the same time. But there was no way I was backing out now.

I wrapped my arms around Quinton and pulled him close to me, groaning when I felt how hard he was for me. We kissed each other frantically as we stumbled into the living room, only pausing long enough to toe-off our shoes. He pushed me back against the wall in the hall and kissed me again. I spun him around and walked him backward into my room. He broke our kiss and opened his eyes for a moment to look around, before pulling me close again.

I walked him to the edge of the bed and crawled up his body as he fell back with a laugh. I stayed on my knees and straddled him, cradling his head in my hands and kissing him until I was sure we'd both have whisker burn tomorrow. But none of that mattered.

I locked eyes with him as I slowly lowered my weight down onto him. My eyes closed on their own accord, and I fought not to press down more than I already was.

He moved his hand to my hip and stilled me. "Keep it up and this is going to be over way sooner than I want it to be."

I smiled down at him as he reached up and gently brushed his fingertips along my jawline.

It felt like everything stopped in that moment. "I know, Enz. We'll be fine, I promise."

"Quinton," he murmured, not breaking eye contact with me.

I nodded around the lump in my throat. "We have too many clothes on."

He grabbed the back of my shirt and pulled it off then flung it aside. His heated gaze took me in before sliding his hands up my chest and brushing his thumbs across my nipples, making me flinch at the shot of electricity that traveled through my body and settled in my groin. I pulled him up by his shoulders, and in a blur of movement and sensation, we were finally naked.

"I want to touch you everywhere," I said, before running my hands down his sides to his firm ass and slowly trailing my fingers across his hole.

"I'm ready, I think I've been waiting for this the whole time we've known each other," he panted out.

I reached over him and took out a condom and lube from the cabinet next to the bed. I wasted no time spreading lube on my fingers and slowly prepping him.

"You're beautiful, Enz, you're the most beautiful man I've ever known. I've wanted you from the first day we met," I rambled, too excited to slow down.

"I want you in me now, don't make me beg."

I slid into him and held myself still for a second, hoping for more control than I seemed capable of. I leaned down and kissed him, so thankful for every touch and sensation with him.

"Make me yours, Q, that's what I've always wanted. Please."

I didn't think of work, or the bakery, or us being partners. In that moment, and for the rest of the night, there was only him. And during one of the many experiences we shared that night, I let myself fall further in love with Enzo, and I didn't feel bad at all.

Eighteen

Enzo

July passed so fast, I barely had time to think about Quinton not being here, but now we were a month closer to the end of our partnership, and after September, he'd be gone.

I sat at my desk in the office and thought of him and smiled. He had very literally rocked my world. I noticed the daily quote on the calendar that sat on my desk: *Memory believes before knowing remembers, William Faulkner Light in August*, it read. I read it over and over and thought back on that July night when I'd felt closer to Quinton than I ever had.

A simple touch and the squeeze of his hand in mine was all it took. After that night, I craved his touch so much, it was always on my mind. I continued to start work early, until finally changing my schedule to accommodate it, and moving a lunch employee to begin his shift earlier so Andrea wasn't left to fend for herself.

Every day I counted how many days remained, and still I couldn't bring myself to be completely honest with Quinton. He deserved to know why I had been so closed off and rude to him, but I wasn't sure I was brave enough to tell him. Or if he'd even care. What if I told him and he thought it was a stupid reason and left anyway? What if he moved far enough away I never saw him again? All because of my own stupidity.

"Hey, Enz, everything okay?" he asked as he peeked around the corner of the door.

"Yeah, just going over some stuff. Nothing too exciting." I tried to smile, but it felt so forced, I knew by the look on his face I didn't fool him at all.

He stepped into the room and squatted down in front of me. "What's going on?" he asked as he cupped my knee with his hand.

I took a deep breath and let it out slowly, trying to find some calm, and maybe a little bit of courage. Finally, after what seemed to take way too long, I answered. "We need to talk, there's so much I need to explain to you. I should have done it years ago, but I just wanted to forget about it."

"You don't owe me anything. I've made my peace with everything that's happened, I just think it's better for us both if I move on and we get a fresh start. It doesn't mean we can't be friends. It just means we're better off not being in business together." He squeezed my knee, seeming to amplify each word with his gentle motion.

I sat for a second, just taking him in; his warm brown eyes seemed to invite me to tell him everything that had been weighing on my conscience for months, if not years. "I have a lot to explain to you, and I want to do that before you leave."

He nodded before he stood and leaned forward to gather me into a hug, which I gratefully accepted and rested my forehead on his shoulder. "Whatever it is, it'll be okay. Don't worry so much, you'll always be my friend," he whispered in my hair.

But I was slowly realizing I didn't want to be his friend; I wanted more. I couldn't pinpoint when that happened, maybe just realizing he wouldn't be around all the time was what it took for me to think about how it would be without him always being there. I had taken him and his friendship for granted. I saw that now. I thought he'd always be there no matter how I treated him or pushed him away.

"I'm so sorry," I whispered to him. I could never make up for all the times I was cold and just plain shitty to him. But I'd try. If he let me, I'd spend the rest of my life making up for all of them. He deserved to be treated so much better than the passive-aggressive crap I threw at him daily. Maybe he was better off without me in his life?

He pulled back and held me at arm's length, then leaned his forehead against mine. "Whatever it is, Enz, we'll work it out." He pulled me back to him and hugged me tight once more before stepping back. "Come on, let's finish up and we can go to my house and talk. Sound good?"

"Yeah, I think that's best. Thanks, Q, for always being such a good friend, even when I wasn't."

He gave me a hard look before nodding and walking back out to the kitchen. After a minute I followed him, and we both got busy stocking the place for breakfast and lunch. I heard Andrea at the door, and I knew this was it. It was time to spill my guts.

I followed him as he drove to his house. It was close to the bakery, only about ten minutes away, but this day I wished it was hours more away, because I dreaded losing my friend, and I didn't want him to see how much of an asshole I really was.

He pulled into his garage, and I followed behind and parked in the driveway. He got out of his car and stood beside it, waiting for me to get out of mine and join him. I couldn't move, though, too afraid of what he'd think when I finally admitted what a dick I was. He waved his hand for me to come on, so I opened the door and followed him into his house.

"So, what did you want to talk about?" Quinton called back over his shoulder as he continued on to his kitchen. "Want some coffee?"

"No, I'm good."

"Okay, so what's this about? I don't have any real suggestions to how you should run the business once I'm gone, if that's what you were wondering."

"No, it's not that. I'm not sure I even want to keep it open once you leave," I admitted.

"What are you talking about? That place was your dream, I thought . . ."

"No, Q, it wasn't my dream. It was a lie. I fucked my dream up before I met you. I wasn't honest with you. When I met you, I had left Portland, where I'd gone to school and had a job that I loved, as a game designer. I was in what I thought was a serious relationship. We'd gone to school together and were working at a tech company as game designers."

"Okay, but I still don't see how this explains anything," he said, confusion clear on his face.

"I had an idea for a game when I was a teenager, and I spent the next three years getting it right. When I wasn't at work, I was working on graphics, writing code, and perfecting my game. And sharing that information with Lane. When I finally had it right and was ready to submit it to the company I worked for, Lane sabotaged it. He rewrote some of the coding and fucked it up. Then after he'd made me look like a fool, he submitted his own version. It worked perfectly, and within two weeks of its public release, it was one of their biggest sellers. He got rich and I got fucked."

"Oh, Enzo, I'm so sorry. I can't imagine, that had to be devastating."

"I'm not gonna lie, it gutted me. Not only did Lane take my game and get all the credit for it, but he threw our relationship away and didn't care. We'd done everything together for six years of my life. When I met you in class that first day, that was my attempt at a new life. I decided I'd go into a business that was as far away from technology as I could get. I had baked all my life as a hobby, but nothing too serious. I also promised myself I'd never trust someone else with my business. But you were always so hardworking and passionate, and so fucking honest."

"I would never have done that to you, you have to know that," Quinton said as he stepped closer to me.

"I know, deep inside I always knew, but my stupid pride got in the way. Every time we had a success at work, I knew I needed to share it with you, and I didn't always want to. Then I kept thinking you would fuck me over. I kept waiting for you to tell me to fuck off, but you never did. And it seemed like once I knew I could get away with it, the worse I treated you. I still don't even know why."

He slid into a chair and put his hand to his forehead as his head fell forward. I reached my hand out to him, but he held his other hand out with his palm facing me. *Stay away*, he seemed to say. "So, you starting a business with me was your second choice. It wasn't your dream, and it wasn't what you actually even wanted for a career. You did it to prove you could do it, and to show up your ex?"

My lip trembled, there was so much hurt and betrayal in his eyes it made my chest ache. "At first it was like that. But the longer we worked together in school, the more I wanted to do it, because I loved working with you. I wanted to make you proud of me. And I wanted us to be in business together."

He stood then. "You need to leave," he said, his voice thick with emotion.

"Wait, Quinton, please. I don't want to lose you."

"You already have. I won't be going back to work while you're there. I'll finish out my time, and only when you're not working. Go, Enzo. I'm done." He stood and walked to the back of his house while I was frozen in shock.

I was such a dick. And I deserved every bad thing that happened because of my own selfish stupidity.

Nineteen

Quinton

Enzo had finally been honest with me, and it wasn't at all what I'd expected to hear. I'd reacted harshly because I realized I didn't know him nearly as well as I thought I did. He had a whole other life before we'd met that he'd never mentioned. Truth be told, I hadn't been honest with him either, but he'd hurt me deeply with his constant bad attitude, and his lack of trust in me. Even when he knew he was hurting me, he didn't stop, and I just ignored it and didn't confront him for fear of never having any chance with him.

He still expected me to leave, to just walk away and leave him and the business behind. I still hadn't told him I'd talked to my dad, and I had a plan that would let us both use the bakery but as separate businesses. I wasn't sure he'd want that, or if he still wanted to be in the bakery business in any capacity.

Well, there was only one way to find out. I'd avoided him long enough. I sent him a text and asked if we could meet up and talk this afternoon. We both worked tonight, so I didn't want either of us to go without the rest we'd need to get through our shift. But I wanted to get this over with. If he didn't like my idea, then hopefully we'd find a way to still be civil until we worked out all the details of what would become of the business. I wasn't sure I could go back to just being friends again.

Nearly as soon as I hit Send, he replied, *I'll be right there. I'll be waiting.*

And just like that, the nerves hit. What if he hated my idea? What if he really did want to close the shop and go into a tech job? What if he didn't feel the same way I did after all, and hadn't known how to tell me?

Images of that night flashed through my mind—him moving under me as I slowly slid into him, then pulling him closer to me so I could pound into him the way I'd dreamed about. The noises he made got me hard just thinking about them. We'd had sex a few times that night, neither of us able to stop what we'd started. Everything with him felt so perfect and natural, like we were made for each other and our bodies knew it.

A knock at the door interrupted my thoughts. I took a deep breath, hoping to calm my body and its instant reaction to everything Enzo. "Hey, come on in," I called to him from the kitchen.

"Hey," he replied as he walked over to me. "I'm so sorry, Quinton, I never did anything with the intention of hurting you. I hope you know that." His eyes pleaded with me for understanding.

"We need to talk, I haven't been honest with you either."

He gave me a look of shock. "What's going on?" he asked as I led him over to the couch so we could sit together while we had this conversation. I couldn't bear to not have him near, and I needed him to know he was important to me above all else.

"After we had our argument—"

"You mean after I treated you like shit and you called me on it."

I couldn't help but smile. "Yeah, that too. Anyway, after that happened, I met with my dad. I decided that I'd like to buy you out. Owning the bakery has been my dream come true. Doing it with you made it that much better, until it didn't. I don't think we can be in business together, but I want to be with you."

"What are you saying?" Enzo choked out, his voice cracking with emotion.

"I want to make a go of a relationship with you." I waited to see what his reaction would be, but he sat quietly and listened. "I don't want to lose you, but I don't think we can be business partners anymore." He nodded and bowed his head. I took his hand, but he looked so defeated, I couldn't stand that I'd made him feel so bad. "Enzo, I think you should start a business with the internet sales. We can work out a deal where we produce food for you, and you run the website and handle orders."

His head snapped up and he met my eyes. Now I could see the tears I couldn't when his head was down. "Do you think that would work?"

"I'm sure it would. We can sell you food that's either fresh or frozen and ready to bake. We can do this, Enzo. We can both work through the bakery but still have our own business. And you can finally use your mad programming skills to make an incredible site for your internet business. So, what do you think?"

He didn't move for a moment as he continued to meet my gaze. "I love that idea. I absolutely love it." He slid closer to me, and when I held my arms out, he melted into them, pressing his face into my neck, before pulling back to meet my gaze.

"Are you sure? I don't want you to feel like I'm taking your business. I'll buy you out, but I really think this could work. I—"

Enzo stopped me with a kiss that I felt in every nerve in my body, and didn't stop until he had covered my face with kisses. I laughed, feeling freer than I had in months. I took his face in my hands and explored his mouth with my tongue until we were both sweaty, panting messes.

I stood and held out my hand. "Come on, let's go to my room."

He jumped up off the couch and practically dragged me down the hall. We could do this, I knew we could.

Twenty

Enzo

A lot had changed since Quinton had asked me over to come clean about not being honest with me. We still saw each other at the shop, but I had my own space a few doors down where I packed orders and organized them for delivery or to be picked up. They made all of the products I sold, but I was in charge of my own menu, and they did their best to make me happy with the items they produced for me. And that wasn't the only change.

"Hey, babe, how's business today?" I asked Quinton as I stepped into the kitchen where he was hard at work on what looked like pie dough.

"Enzo, are you done with work already?"

"Yep, I went in early, have everything ready for delivery, and I was hoping we could do something this afternoon."

Andrea looked at me and smiled, and I gave her a little wave. I missed working with her, but I didn't miss the hours. Even Quinton had stopped working so early. Now he went in at four, which was still early, but at least he wasn't staying up all night and part of the day.

"I think I could manage that. What do you have in mind?"

"Well it's going to be a beautiful day, how about going to Apple Hill? We can pick out a pumpkin for Halloween and try some apple treats."

He wiped his hands off on his apron as he approached me, then put his hand to my cheek. I immediately covered it with mine. I'd never get tired of this. How had we worked together for so long and not realized how perfect we were for each other? Maybe we were blinded by the job, or maybe we were both too stubborn. And while I felt guilty for how badly I'd treated Quinton, I was so thankful that he called me on my bullshit and made me look at things through different eyes.

I loved him more than I would have thought possible, and I knew he felt the same. I was stupid and so blind for too many years. It had been a whole year since we had split up as business partners, but also a year of us being officially boyfriends. We hadn't had a single fight since then. It seemed all we needed to do was to not be in business together and everything worked.

"That sounds great, I have a few apple recipes I've been waiting to try. So, once again, your timing is perfect." He punctuated his answer with a kiss, and Andrea moved to the front of the bakery, making herself busy and giving us some privacy.

"How much later are you working?" I asked.

He looked up at the clock and then seemed to think about what he needed to have finished before leaving for the day. "I can leave now. Andrea will only be here for about an hour by herself, until the new guy arrives to help her out."

"That okay with you, Andrea?" I shouted toward the front.

She popped her head around the doorway to look at me. "Of course, you two go and have fun. Enjoy the great weather," she said with a wink.

Quinton looked between her and I before pulling me into his arms. "What was that wink? Do you two have something planned that I don't know about?"

"Nope, no idea what you're talking about." I struggled to look innocent, but he'd been suspicious for weeks. He knew something was going on, but I hoped he didn't know what I had planned.

I had decided about a month ago that I'd ask Quinton to marry me. Since he had been the one who had made that first move a year ago, I wanted to be the one who took us to the next step.

I'd talked to one of the farmers Quinton bought produce from at the markets he now frequented. When I told him my idea, he was more than willing to help me make it happen. I'd driven up there early this morning and set up a table in the vineyard with the backdrop of apple trees that were now loaded with fruit. I also ordered us lunch to be delivered as soon as we arrived.

If everything went as planned, I'd be on my knee and asking this wonderful man to be mine forever. Just imagining it made me smile.

"What's got you smiling?"

"Nothing, just glad we get to have a day off together." He didn't seem convinced, but he smiled back at me, and within twenty minutes we were on the road. I patted my pocket, checking once again for the ring I hoped he'd love. I was so excited I could barely contain myself, so instead I rambled all the way to the exit for Apple Hill.

Twenty-One

Quinton

He thought he was so sneaky, making plans for Apple Hill, and who knew what else. Well I had a surprise for him too. I'd decided that it was time for us to make our relationship official. I'd bought a ring, and while we were at an apple orchard, enjoying the beauty of fall, I'd ask him to marry me.

The past year had been filled with so many new emotions, but overwhelmingly it had been filled with our love. Every time we touched, or our eyes met, I was reminded of our deep connection and how much we meant to each other. We'd never own a business together again, our relationship was too important, but we'd be together, hopefully forever. He had my heart, and in a little while, he'd have my ring.

I drove as we left Sacramento and headed toward the Placerville area. Apple Hill was beautiful anytime of the year, but fall was my favorite. I listened quietly as Quinton rambled the whole way there. He talked about everything and nothing all at once, and I enjoyed every second.

I couldn't believe how much there still was to learn about him. We'd been friends before, but now we were so much more. I loved getting to know him more personally and found every little new discovery fascinating and . . . sweet. He really was a very sweet and passionate man. Just not with baking. His business was an instant success. People loved the food we produced, and his flawless delivery service made us all look good. His website was so popular that he rarely needed to advertise, but he did it anyway just because he enjoyed it.

I looked forward to spending more time with him. We didn't live together, but we may as well have. He was at my house or I was at his nearly every night. Once we'd admitted our feelings, neither of us wanted to be apart for one more night.

My mind wandered as he continued to ramble about anything and everything. I took the main exit for Apple Hill and we made our way along the narrow road that led to the many farms there. Most were apple farms, but there were more things to look at than apples now.

"Where do you want to start?" I asked.

"Let's just pull into the first one. The weather's so nice today, I want to see it all," Enzo said.

"Your wish is my command."

"Oh, I might take you up on that later." He smiled at me while reaching for my hand as I pulled over to the side of the road, next to the first farm. We both walked around and looked at everything they had to see, including pumpkins of every size and variety, crates of fresh-picked apples, and every combination of apple dessert imaginable.

I walked over to the bakery area to see if anything there inspired me to add it to the menu. There were so many options. I closed my eyes and inhaled the cinnamon-and-apple goodness. I felt Enzo step up behind me and trail his hand down my arm to my fingers before weaving them together. I turned my head to look at him.

"You almost ready to move on to the next place? Or did you want to try something here?"

I took a step forward and spun around to face him, while walking backward, still holding his hand. "I'm ready to go, let's see what else there is to see."

We stopped at several farms, and each one had a different theme even though they were all basically selling the same thing; no two of them were alike. I felt so relaxed, probably more than I had in months. We drove past a few that were either closed, or didn't look like something we'd be interested in. Finally, we came to a winery, the surrounding fields covered with neat lines of grapevines, and fruit trees all neatly laid out around a large grassy area.

"Can we go here?" Enzo asked.

"Yeah, this is beautiful."

"I thought so too," he mumbled almost too quietly for me to hear.

"What was that?"

"Oh, look, they have a tasting room. Come on, let's go." As soon as the car pulled to a stop, Enzo was out of the car and standing at the front of it, waiting for me. I patted my pocket one more time just to be sure. I was still waiting to find that perfect place to ask Enzo the question that had been burning on my lips all day.

"This way, I want to see what's over here," Enzo said as he pulled me along the side of one of the buildings on the farm.

"Enzo, are you sure about this?" I asked, thinking there was no way he knew where he was leading me, and was just planning on wandering the property.

He stopped and turned, giving me a serious look. "I'm sure. I'm so sure." He turned then and continued to drag me along behind him.

Twenty-Two

Enzo

I was so excited I could barely contain myself. As soon as Quinton pulled into the parking lot, I wanted to run to the orchard where everything was set up and waiting for us. The entire time we'd been wandering around the other farms, I'd been texting with the owner of the winery, who was more than happy to make this day even more special. I had also talked to him about my online store, and he seemed interested. I hoped that I could talk to him more about it later, but that would be much later. Right now I needed to focus on Quinton.

"Where are you taking me, Enz?"

"You'll see, come on." I practically dragged him along, but I couldn't seem to stop myself. I was so excited and anxious to see what the owner had come up with. I was also anxious to see Quinton's reaction. I patted my pocket once again, and continued along the dirt road that led toward the fields and vineyards.

We walked a little farther, and I saw ribbons tied to the grapevines, just like I'd been told they would be. Quinton didn't seem to notice them, or if he did, he didn't mention them. But when I looked back at him, he was grinning from ear to ear, and I couldn't stop myself from smiling back at him.

The rows of grapevines curved along with the soft rolling hills we walked on, and when we were past the curve, I could see the small table I'd set up earlier. Right there in the middle of the grapes. Complete with a crisp white tablecloth, chairs that were also draped in white fabric, a large market umbrella, and an ice bucket that held a bottle of Quinton's favorite wine.

"Enz, what's this?"

I turned then and took both his hands in mine. "I wanted to do something special for you. For us."

"I'd say you accomplished it, this is amazing." He tried to move past me to the table, but I held fast to his hands. He looked away from the table and met my eyes, a look of confusion on his handsome face. "Enz?"

"Quinton, you mean more to me than I could ever say. I love you, you're my heart. Even though we've proven we cannot be business partners, I'm hoping that you'd like to be another type of partner with me." I let go of his left hand and reached into my pocket to retrieve the ring, then quickly dropped to one knee.

"Are you saying what I think you're saying?"

"If you think I'm asking you to marry me, then yes, you're right."

He beamed down at me, his beautiful eyes bright with emotion. He let go of my hand and dug in his own pocket, before he dropped to his knee right in front of me.

"What are you—?"

"Enzo, I love you. You have been the toughest nut to crack, but you finally showed me your soft center. And I love what I see. Will you marry me?"

For a moment, I wasn't sure if I should laugh, or if he was being serious. But looking into his eyes, I knew the answer.

He stayed there, frozen, hand out and clutching a small black box. My gaze bounced between the box and his face. "Yes, yes, oh god, yes." I dove at him and kissed every part of him I could reach, before I realized he had yet to answer me. "Hey, wait, what's *your* answer?"

His smile grew even brighter as he held my face in both his hands, like I was the most precious thing he'd ever seen. "Yes, Enz, always yes." He took my hand and slid a ring on my finger; it was platinum with a ribbon of gold and black woven across the top of it. Perfect. And then he was kissing me again, until we were both breathless and laughing as we cried tears of joy. It was the most perfect moment that could have ever been. But I realized every moment with Quinton was a perfect moment, and after today, we'd have an infinite amount of perfect moments to share.

"By the way, nice proposal," Quinton said.

"Thanks, Andrea helped me out."

"I'm sure she did."

"Now come on, fiancé, let's see go enjoy our meal and toast to our engagement."

I took his hand, but he pulled me back to him. "Did you forget something?"

"Nope, you're not getting your ring until dessert. Anticipation is everything," I said with a wink as I pulled the chair out for him.

As we sat in that vineyard, toasting our engagement and examining both our rings, I thought I was the luckiest guy ever—to love someone who loved me back just as much, and was possibly the best friend I'd ever had.

THE END

About The Author

BL Maxwell grew up in a small town listening to her grandfather spin tales about his childhood. Later she became an avid reader and after a certain vampire series she became obsessed with fanfiction. She soon discovered Slash fanfiction and later discovered the MM genre and was hooked. Many years later, she decided to take the plunge and write down some of the stories that seem to run through her head late at night when she's trying to sleep.

Contact:

Email: blmaxwell.writer@gmail.com
blmaxwellwriter.com
https://smart.bio/blmaxwellwriter/

Also By BL Maxwell

Thank you for reading Six Months, be sure to check out other books in the Small Town City Series

SMALL TOWN CITY series

https://mybook.to/SmallTownCity
Remember When
A Night to Remember (Short Story) Free Read
Try To Forget

Try To Remember (Short Story)
One Last Chance

Green Eyed Boy, Lobster Tales Book One, is available Here:

https://mybook.to/GreenEyedBoy

Two strangers, drawn together over their work ethic, and sealing the deal over delicious lobster rolls. They could just be the perfect match.
After quitting his job, Billie Watts hits all the food festivals he can as he drives across the country. When he finally reaches Stoney Brook, Maine, he's excited to find he's there just in time to try one of the lobster rolls he's heard so much about. The bright neon yellow food truck with a giant red lobster on top looks like the perfect place to try it.
Lance Karl is as ready as he can be for the start of the three-day Tall Ships Festival and hopes to sell enough lobster rolls out of his food truck to make a good start towards owning a restaurant. The day begins cold and misty, and a text from his nephew saying he can't help him is not the perfect start he'd hoped for.
When a green-eyed stranger interrupts his frantic morning, Lance doesn't realize meeting Billie will not only change his day, but maybe even the rest of his life. Two strangers, drawn together over their work ethic, and sealing the deal over delicious lobster rolls. They could just be the perfect match. A small-town MM Vacation romance.#friends to lovers #meet-cute #workplace romance #mm romance

Enjoy a Free copy of Try To Remember. A short story with Andy and Link.

https://blmaxwellwriter.com/free-reads/
And a Free copy of A Night To Remember. A short story with Sam and Erik.

https://books2read.com/u/baDrw8

Preorder The Things We Lose: https://mybook.to/TTWLose

BETTER TO-GETHER series

Better Together
Chains Required
The First Twelve
The Better Together Boxset

THE STONE series

Stone Under Skin
Blood Beneath Stone
Stone Hearts
The Stone Series Box Set

VALLEY GHOSTS series

Series Link: mybook.to/ValleyGhostsSeries
Ghost Hunted
Ghost Haunted

Ghost Trapped
Ghost Hexed
Ghost Handled
Ghost Shadow
Haunting Destiny

CONSORTIUM TRILOGY

Burning Addiction
Freezing Aversion

FOUR PACKS Trilogy

The Slow Death
The Ultimate Sacrifice
The Final Salvation

STANDALONE

The List
Double Black Diamonds
Ride: The Chance of a Lifetime
Check Yes or No
A Ghost of a Chance
Tutu
Salt & Lime
Amos Ridge
Six Months
Ten or Fifteen Miles
The Snake in the Castle
Green Eyed Boy
A Beach Far Away
The Things We Find
Blinding Light

Peppermint Mocha Kisses

Small Town City Series

Remember When

BL Maxwell

https://mybook.to/RememberWhenA
A night to remember, a confession, and a lifetime of love in this small town, friends to lovers Christmas romance.
Andrew Lawson's life in Sacramento has turned from being everything he dreamed of growing up, to a lonely place where finding someone special to share his life with is impossible. When the first person he meets on returning home for Thanksgiving is his childhood friend Link, it's a reminder of happier times when his whole future lay in front of him. Agreeing to a drink before heading to his parent's place is a way to reconnect, and a great way to start the holiday.
Link Stanton never considered leaving the small farming town he grew up in, but he misses Andy more than he'll ever admit. Secretly lusting after a friend is bad enough but being in love with him is so much worse. One drink with friends seems harmless enough, after all, catching up on old times can't be a bad thing, until beers turn to shots, and Link reveals how he really feels.
Everything could change, and if Andrew doesn't remember Link's heartfelt confession, they could carry on as friends. But, if he does remember, this could be either the worst, or the best, Christmas of all. #smalltownromance #Holidayromance #mmromance #Christmas #friendstolovers

Try To Forget

BL Maxwell

https://mybook.to/TryToForget
After being dumped by his boyfriend, spending the weekend
alone wasn't something Sam Braun was looking forward to.
So, when the hairstylist that works next to his bookstore
invites him to his hometown for the weekend, Sam jumps at
the chance. Visiting the small town of Occident could be just
what he needs to forget, at least for a few days.
Erik Thorne has lived his whole life in the same town where
nothing new ever happens, and any stranger who comes to
town is always a big deal. When his old friend Andy brings
a friend home for the weekend, Erik is drawn to the man in
a way that confuses him at first. But his curiosity about the
gorgeous blond from the city gets the better of him, and he
can't resist spending more time with him.
Sam was hoping to forget his troubles when he meets Erik.
While Erik can't seem to think of anything besides the city
boy with the bookstore he can't wait to visit. Distance might
not be the only thing that stands between them, as they
find out admitting what you want isn't always easy. Each
book can be read as a standalone. #AgeGap, #MMRomance,
#FriendsToLovers #OppositesAttract #SmallTownRomance
#City/Country

One Last Chance (New Release)

https://mybook.to/OLCSmalltown
Stu Lawson had always lived in the small town of Occident.
He'd been born a farmer, and he was more than happy to stay
a farmer even when his dad decided it wasn't the life for him.
He's been raising his daughter since the day she was born,

and he's never regretted being a single dad, but Stu has a few secrets.

Morgan Grant was born into a life he never wanted and had done everything he could to avoid. Staying drunk helps him forget and numbs the pain he can't bring himself to face. After a long night of drinking, he ends up dumped in a small town north of Sacramento without money, his phone, or a way to get back to the city he calls home.

Stu's focus has always been his daughter, but he can't control his curiosity about the stranger who shows up in Occident alone in the middle of the night. He offers to help, even when he knows he shouldn't. Old feelings rise to the surface and he's helpless to ignore them, or Morgan. This stranger could be his chance at happiness, or his downfall. #singledad #gayromance #stranded #smalltownromance #secrets

Peppermint Mocha Kisses

https://mybook.to/PeppermintMK

Randy Miller wants nothing more than to make a living selling the fantastic cookies he dreams up when he's not working as a web designer. He's always loved baking, but he's afraid of taking the leap from hobby to business. Mostly he's afraid of failing, and of Eli coming up with a better recipe.

Eli Canton has a crush. A big crush on someone who avoids him whenever he can. Eli loves everything about Randy, even if he's grouchy and seems to work way too much. Eli knows he's not all bad and hopes to have a chance with him someday. A broken oven throws the two of them together, and even though Randy doesn't want to admit it, he likes the time he spends with Eli. And Eli definitely can't wait to spend more time with Randy. Now if only they can make it past the annual cookie exchange and possibly Valentine's Day to their own sweet happy ending. #smalltown Romance, #opposites attract, #MM Romance

The Ultimate Sacrifice (Four Packs Trilogy Book 2)

https://mybook.to/FourPacksTrilogy
Grady Summerville is facing a slow and agonizing death, but has come to terms with his disease and doesn't fear dying. However, fate has other ideas, presenting him with a future thanks to Max Steele. Grady owes his very life to Max, and as his health improves, finds himself falling head over heels with his savior.

Max Steele has been forced to leave his pack and everyone he knows to move to the West Territory to be a blood donor for Grady. He knows it's the right thing to do, but it doesn't mean he has to like it.
As tensions escalate between the two packs, Max finds his loyalty tested and is torn between following his alpha, or following his heart.
If Max doesn't make the sacrifice then it will be Grady making the ultimate sacrifice and paying with his life. #MMParanormal #Shifters

Freezing Aversion (Consortium Trilogy Book Two)

The cold isn't the only killer in the wilderness.

https://mybook.to/FreezingAversion

Benjamin Coulton is a tracker employed by the Consortium, the ruling counsel of vampires. When he's sent to investigate a rogue vampire killing indiscriminately in a remote region of Alaska. Bad weather hampers his effort and he loses the vampire he's been tasked to find.
Leon Davis and his friend Trevor agreed to be winter caretakers for several cabins and a fishing lodge, thinking it would be easy money. They settle into their daily routine of checking the cabins for animal break-ins, or broken water pipes, and prepare for a long winter.
Until a run in with a vampire changes everything.
Ben finds a newly turned vampire left for dead by the rogue vampire, and suddenly Ben's mission changes course. In the freezing wilderness of Alaska, he uncovers more truths and the mate he'd always longed for... and now the vampire he was tasked to find is hunting them. #MMParanormalRomance #vampire #fatedmate #thriller

A Ghost of a Chance

https://mybook.to/AGhostOfAChance
James McKinney has always lived life alone. He doesn't have a family, at least none that he remembers. He's always dreamed of having a house of his own, a place he can call home. Finding the right house, ready to work to make it his home, nothing can put a damper on his happiness, or can it?Trey Andral, returning home from college, notices someone moving into his old friend's house next door. Miss Hattie is still waving to him from the bedroom window, even though he knows

she's gone. He also knows he can't not help the new guy make the house his own.Trey has always been able to see and hear sprits, but what's normal to him is terrifying to most others. When the spirits seem intent on contacting James, Trey has no choice but to share his secret, risking their friendship. If they work together, maybe they can figure out what the clues the spirits are giving them mean. And maybe they can find family in each other.

Tutu (Malicious Gods: Egypt)

https://mybook.to/Tutu

Kit Nelson was thrown into the world of demons and cults as a child. He's learned to depend on no one, and to do all he can to keep himself safe from dark forces. He also knows he can't trust anyone else with his life. He knows what the demons who hunt him have in mind for him, and he'll fight it every step of the way.

Tommy Smythe and his sister Lola have been fighting what they know is a rising tide of evil for years. They're prepared with all their paranormal weaponry, including the assistance of an ancient god who has fought demons his whole existence.

Tutu, the Egyptian god and Master of Demons has chosen Tommy to be his vessel and his sword when needed to destroy any and all demons.

A new threat ripples through the dark underworld, one that will be felt across all mankind. A demon has chosen one whose body he will use to return to the land of the living. But only if Kit, Tommy, and Lola can't stop him. Only Tutu has the power and knowledge to protect them from the demon Rerek, and he also knows even with his help, this is not going to be an easy battle.

Amos Ridge

https://mybook.to/AmosRidge

"There's no time. Remember, I love you."It all started with a discovery. A cave beneath a waterfall that held a crystal. Two boys—best friends—embark on a journey they're told will help all mankind. As the years go by, their friendship turns to love, and their adventure turns into a battle.Drew Langly is the keeper of the crystal. With his contact, the crystal allows them to jump to different timestreams and help, if they can, to further that society or fix anything that improves their lives. When he's ripped from the timestream, it's the beginning of what will change everything they've come to know about how the different timestreams function.Colby Adams is Drew's boyfriend, fellow traveler, and jump partner. When Drew is left vulnerable after a failed jump, he's there to help and try to figure out what went wrong. They soon discover another team of travelers is in trouble, but they've been warned against trusting them. The more they learn, the more they realize everything has been a lie. To rewrite a history that's been full of deceit, they'll need to put their trust, once again, in strangers. Can they rewind it all and begin again? Experience the history they were always meant to? With some unconventional help, maybe...

Blinding Light

Please enjoy the first chapter of Blinding Light.

Easy

"Easy, get yer ass over here," Vance yelled at me from across the studio. We'd been working hard to get ready for Rocktoberfest, and—we still needed a lot of work.

"Yeah, what is it?" Vance stood there with a guy that was hot as hell. White, blond hair, and lots of tattoos, just my kinda guy. "Hey," I said, and tried to keep it cool in case he wasn't here just for my entertainment.

"He's not here for that. This is Liam Tarrant, he's the new guitarist and here to help with vocals." Vance stood there with his hands resting on his hips daring me to say something. He'd been our manager since the beginning of Blinding Light ten years ago and was just as much a dick then as he was now.

"We don't need help with vocals." I crossed my arms and ignored the new guy.

"Well, you're getting it. Management hired him, and you'll work with him. Besides, he's going to replace Jake. He's done." Without a backward glance, he walked off and slammed the door to his office. I stared at the door he'd just closed and avoided looking at the new guy who had yet to say a word.

"Did you bring your instrument?" I finally asked, annoyed as hell and not feeling bad at all for taking it out on the new guy.

He nodded and turned around, moving back to the door Vance had walked through. A moment later he returned carrying a guitar case. He marched up to me but still hadn't said a word. Not that I minded. It was better than endless chatter about nothing. "This way." I turned and led him to the practice room. The others were already there. "This is the new guy. Liam, meet the rest of the band. That's Glen on drums, and Rory on bass."

"Hey, man," they both mumbled. We'd been through this a few times, actually I'd been through it. Glen was the longest founding member besides me and he'd left a few times and come back. Rory joined us three years ago, and we'd recently lost Jake the guitarist.

Liam went over to one of the amps and proceeded to plug in and warm up. I leaned against my own amp and Glen and Rory stopped to watch. He warmed up with a few simple chords before ripping into a screaming solo that was far better than any guitarist we'd had in a while.

"That's all well and good, but can you play *our* songs?" I set a mic stand in front of him; if he was going to play he was going to sing too, no matter how much I hated it. I hadn't been able to hit all the notes for a few years, but luckily for me the gravel in my voice helped me hide a lot of that.

His eyes locked on mine as he leaned back, one foot forward, guitar slung higher than most, and played. His fingers flew over the strings, as his lips moved with the music and rhythm. Those lips . . . plump, pink. Definitely kissable. I shook my head to get back to listening. He started playing 'Give Up The Love', one of our hits. As his fingers flew over the strings leading up to the chorus, Glen pounded out the rhythm, and Rory joined on bass.

I stepped up to the mic and ripped it out of the stand. "Give up, give up the love. You know you've got to give up, give up the love." I sang, while the three of them fell into a rhythm as though they'd been playing together for years rather than one song.

But then he stepped up to my side and leaned his back against me as he harmonized with me. His voice was a perfect match for mine. The voice I'd had before too many cigarettes, and a few beers. His heat was intense against my side, and when he leaned away to turn and play it up with Rory, I found I missed it. He was good, *really* good, and when Glen met my eyes over the cymbals, his grin told me he felt the same way.

I belted out the next few lines and watched as Liam played the whole song without missing a note and sang without being prompted. He was perfect. So fucking perfect, and I hated him. "That's great, man, can you wait outside the room so we can talk?"

With a tight smile, he walked out and pulled the door shut behind him.

"So, what do you guys think?" I asked, even though I knew the answer.

"Are you fucking kidding me? He tore up the solo, and his vocals are on point. We need to grab him before someone else does." Glen was the first to speak up, and I wasn't surprised at his excitement.

"What do you think?" I asked Rory.

"I just want to play. He's great, he knew 'Give Up The Love' better than the last two guitarists did and they were both with us for a while," Rory said as he plucked at the strings of his bass.

Fuck. I knew it, and I agreed. "We have a week until we start the tour that will take us to Rocktoberfest, then we'll have two months off before we start again. Do you think this guy can handle it?"

"How the fuck do we know?" Rory said. "Jake left us the night before the last gig, as long as this guy doesn't bail on us like he did, I'm happy to give him a chance."

Fucking Jake, it had been three weeks since he'd decided he was done with the music industry and left us all high and dry without looking back. "He's young, has he even played in a band before?" I knew I was being an ass, but I didn't want to keep playing this game of changing band members anymore.

"He has." Vance walked into the room and gave me a scowl. "He just left Vibrancy; they were going in a different direction, and he didn't want to do that. He likes playing hard rock and wanted to stick with it. We're lucky to have gotten a chance at him before another band snatches him up, and they will. You saw him play, he's a musical genius. You need to get your ego out of the decision, his voice and yours together will sound like magic, and his guitar skills are untouchable. Sorry, Rory."

Rory held his hands up. "No offense taken; I agree he's amazing. What are we waiting for, Easy?"

"I just want to be sure, he's a kid. What does he know about sticking around until we finish the tour? And why would he care if we make all the dates or not? He could leave any time and leave us stranded again without a guitarist." We'd had to cancel after Jake left, three shows that were highly anticipated, and that we were hoping gave us a big push in publicity leading up to Rocktoberfest, but that was all gone now.

"I wouldn't do that." We all spun around at the sound of an unfamiliar voice to find Liam standing inside the door. "I take my work very seriously, and I appreciate the chance I'm being given. I won't jeopardize that." His voice was deep and smooth and I struggled not to focus on how much other parts of me responded to him as he spoke.

"Then you're in, now get in here. We need to practice if we're not going to totally blow it at Rocktoberfest." He smiled, and my god. I turned back to my mic stand, mostly to get him out of my head for a second. "Let's do this!"

Glen hit his sticks together and with the bass leading us, we started playing the next song on the playlist.

Blinding Light: https://mybook.to/BlindingLight
Preorder Faded Dreams: https://mybook.to/FadedDreamsR
TR2

About the Author

BL Maxwell grew up in a small town listening to her grandfather spin tales about his childhood. Later she became an avid reader and after a certain vampire series she became obsessed with fanfiction. She soon discovered Slash fanfiction and later discovered the MM genre and was hooked. Many years later, she decided to take the plunge and write down some of the stories that seem to run through her head late at night when she's trying to sleep.

Contact:

Email: blmaxwell.writer@gmail.com

https://smart.bio/blmaxwellwriter/